big babies

VEL)

HOLLYWOOD

IF OUR STORY POINTS
UP ANY MORAL, I
THINK IT'S THAT
YOU CAN'T GET
THROUGH LIFE WITHOUT
ENCOUNTERING AT
LEAST TWO VIOLENTLY
UNSTABLE PEOPLE—AND
THAT'S JUST IN
YOUR FAMILY.

Sherwood Kiraly

AUTHOR OF *DIMINISHED CAPACITY*

MORE PRAISE FOR SHERWOOD KIRALY

DIMINISHED CAPACITY

"Kiraly captivates the reader with both his comic Midwestern sensibility and an eye for small-town absurdities. *Diminished Capacity* has it all: action, adventure, romance, and one amazingly preserved baseball card."

—Mark Steven Johnson, screenwriter,
Grumpy Old Men

"Funny, utterly guileless and friendly . . . This is a fast, light book meant to be simply enjoyed. But unlike so many novels of a similar type, *Diminished Capacity* is extremely well written and has a real message about faith and courage. Cooper and Rollie are original characters . . . A truly good-hearted novel."

—*Los Angeles Times*

"Engaging, quirky . . . good for a laugh and a pleasant afternoon."

—*Publishers Weekly*

CALIFORNIA RUSH

"Comically profound."

—*The Boston Globe*

"An appealing triple play: a likable narrator, a cast of zany characters and a great, albeit unbelievable, story to tell. He manages to capture perfectly the essence of Midwestern club farm teams and exhibits some excruciatingly funny dialogue in this his first novel. A fun, quick read." —*Pittsburgh Press*

"A rare treat . . . Sherwood Kiraly has swept a literary double-header. Not only has he written a delightful first novel, he has also written a delightful baseball novel . . . A whimsical, light and loving look at baseball, and the author gets special applause."

—*St. Louis Post Dispatch*

"A wonderfully told story, with well-drawn characters and a nice turn of phrase."

—*Library Journal*

Berkley Books by Sherwood Kiraly

DIMINISHED CAPACITY
BIG BABIES

BIG BABIES

A NOVEL
SHERWOOD KIRALY

BERKLEY BOOKS, NEW YORK

"*Blah, Blah, Blah,*" music and lyrics by George Gershwin and Ira Gershwin.
© 1931 (Renewed) WB Music Corp.
All Rights Reserved. Used by Permission.
WARNER BROS. PUBLICATIONS U.S. INC., Miami, FL. 33014

"*They Can't Take That Away From Me,*" music and lyrics by George Gershwin and Ira Gershwin.
© 1936, 1937 (Renewed 1963, 1964) George Gershwin Music and Ira Gershwin Music.
All rights administered by WB Music Corp.
All Rights Reserved. Used by Permission.
WARNER BROS. PUBLICATIONS U.S. INC., Miami, FL. 33014

BIG BABIES

A Berkley Book / published by arrangement with the author

PRINTING HISTORY
Berkley trade paperback edition / November 1996

The Putnam Berkley World Wide Web site address is
http://www.berkley.com/berkley

ISBN: 0-425-15457-2

BERKLEY®
Berkley Books are published by The Berkley Publishing Group, 200 Madison Avenue, New York, New York 10016.
BERKLEY and the "B" design
are trademarks belonging to Berkley Publishing Corporation.

PRINTED IN THE UNITED STATES OF AMERICA

10 9 8 7 6 5 4 3 2 1

BIG BABIES

PROLOGUE

Dear Irene Galowicz Otto:

I recently discovered that you are my birth mother. I don't want to disturb you after all these years, but I have a request.

They have a system now in Illinois where an adoptee with a medical need can apply to have his adoption records opened. Then, if a judge agrees, a confidential intermediary contacts the birth parent and asks for whatever medical information the adoptee needs.

That's not how I got your name, but it's one of the reasons I'm writing. I have a five-year-old daughter. She had the croup when she was two—so did I—and she and I have the same palms: wrinkly and red, with very thin skin. Since we share our croup history and our palms, we might share other conditions. I was wondering if you might, at your convenience, send a note mentioning any outstanding ailments you or my birth father have had that Maggie might need to know about as she gets older.

Other than that, I'm writing because this is the first chance I've ever had. You don't have to answer, or meet me. In fact, to tell you the truth, recent events involving my brother Sterling have made it clear to me that there's a lot to be said for leaving things the way they are.

You don't know Sterling, but you may have seen him last week on CNN. He's the guy who went flying over the Las Vegas Strip on New Year's Eve in the Little Spudge-Face Baby Safety Suit and got shot by his biological brother. Afterward, in the ICU, very much on Demerol, Sterling said he had the whole nature-nurture controversy worked out. All the percentages, as he put it. He also said he believes Frank Faylen, who played Dobie Gillis's father, and John Mahoney, who now plays Frasier Crane's father, are the same person. The doctors said his condition was serious, which you could figure out by just listening to him.

Sterling's story and mine are entwined. He was there on the Strip because of me. The very day after the flight and the shooting, I got offers from two of those TV talk shows on which the guests make spectacles of themselves. Sterling and I were supposed to appear together, assuming he pulled through, and tell our tale: sort of "adoptive brothers meet biological brothers at the OK Corral."

I turned the offers down on Sterling's behalf. He never wanted to go on TV as himself. His great wish was to get back on TV and say just one line right as an actor, to make up for his disaster on "Manhattan Live" years ago. The truth is, when the gunmen showed up on the Strip that night, my first thought was, This is going to make Sterling blow his line.

Although I don't want to tell our story on TV, I do feel a compulsion, now that I've learned your name, to tell it to you. It may run a little long, but you and I never got to write each other, so I kind of thought, well, I can do my side of the correspondence here, all in one go.

You owe me nothing back. I don't have any requests beyond the medical one I made above, for Maggie. I just want to let you know what happened since you last saw me. I hope you'll be interested in how I turned out. If afterward you should want to write, that would be fine. But don't feel obliged to meet me. Maybe we could just exchange photos. This whole thing with Sterling has turned me around on the subject of reunions.

If our story points up any moral, I think it's that you can't get through life without encountering at least two violently unstable people—and that's just in your family. When our situation boiled over the other night, it occurred to me that I'd been expecting something like it ever since I was about ten. I'll say this: I hope that was it. I mean I hope that was all of it. I've had enough to last me. From now on I'd like to just sit out back and change the string on the Weedwhacker.

Anyway, here goes. I feel awkward writing this. I keep picturing a gray-haired lady reading it.

Maybe I'll get more comfortable as I go along. I apologize in advance for any offensive language I may use when quoting, or just telling what happened.

My name is Adlai Jerome Fleger. I go by A.J.

CHAPTER ONE

Sterling and I were adopted two years apart by Paul and Rita Fleger in the mid-fifties. Sterling is exactly two years older than me; we have a coincidental birthday, March 3. When we were four and two, the Flegers moved from the South Side of Chicago to Henley, a western suburb which was notable because it didn't have any bad neighborhoods. It had rich sections and okay sections. Mom and Dad made a down payment in an okay section, two blocks from the Burlington depot.

Dad took the train into the Loop to an accounting job every weekday, and Mom drove to the South Side, where she worked as a secretary for a doctor. We stayed home with Grandma Jessie, Mom's mom.

We always knew we were adopted. Mom explained that we were lucky because she and Dad had picked us out specially. They didn't give us details about you or any other birth parents. They used to tell us they were going to give us back to the Indians, but that was a kidding expression and not a clue.

They did reveal that Sterling and I weren't related biologically. We would have suspected this anyway. Sterling grew up big and burly, with curly brown hair, a high forehead and a jutting jaw. He could've dug a hole in the yard with his chin. I was short, skinny and pale. He got good grades through high school and worked hard for them. He played hard too; he'd go till he dropped. My grades were passable but I was much less energetic. Grandma Jessie told me sloth was one of the seven deadly sins, but it didn't seem as deadly to me as some of the others. In the family photos I'm always standing back, watching somebody else do something.

We asked Mom a few times about our "real parents," but the phrase hurt her feelings, so after a while we dropped the subject. When I was little and having a tantrum I used to say I wanted to go back to my real parents, but it was just something I said because I was mad. I really didn't want to change for something unknown.

At school, the kids in both Sterling's class and mine were told at some point to draw their family tree. I drew the Fleger tree, as it had been told to me, including Grandpa Clifford, who killed himself in the Depression. Sterling just drew himself, flamboyantly, with muscles and a bazooka—he preferred to see himself as a glorious original.

Sometimes—rarely—as an exercise, I would

clench my brain and knot my forehead and strain to see a picture from the time before I came home with Mom and Dad, but I never saw anything.

Being adopted didn't make me feel bad. I'd like to stress that, in case you've ever worried about it. The soap operas we watched with Grandma Jessie in the summer often featured tortured adoptees in the plot line, desperate to find out who their father was, and later discovering he was running for governor. Sterling and I felt these adoptee characters were overdramatic and crudely played.

He and I spoke once about becoming detectives someday and locating our blood parents, but the idea fizzled out as we got older. When Sterling was in high school, he said he didn't want to find them anymore. He said if he didn't know who his natural parents were, then he was free to be anybody. He had observed that the kids who knew their natural parents didn't seem uniformly pleased.

When we wanted to indulge ourselves, we had access to romantic fantasies unavailable to the majority of kids. I imagined a birth father who spent his time in foreign lands, toppling repressive governments. Sterling intended to become famous someday and figured his blood parents, Lee Marvin and Angie Dickinson, would contact him later, when he was prominent.

I also assumed Sterling was destined for greatness because throughout elementary school his teachers, who became my teachers, recalled him as special. They would ask if I was Sterling Fleger's little brother, and remark—with a flicker of disappointment—on how different we were. In third grade I responded, "That's because I'm a bastard," a word Sterling had used to explain why we looked different from each other and everybody else in the family.

I envied Sterling, and we argued incessantly, but I also admired him. At school, standing in his shadow, I could smart off to bigger kids, confident that he had a punch like the kick of a pony. Away from school he was responsible for me too. If the two of us got put on the Burlington to go into Chicago and meet Dad at Union Station, it was Sterling who gave the conductor the tickets and did all the worrying. I never worried when I was with him.

Since both Mom and Dad worked, the daily home team was Sterling, me, and Grandma Jessie, who took care of us and the laundry and house-cleaning. She was tiny and white-haired and dressed in floral and polka-dot outfits. She loved her daughter and grandsons, but her devotion to family didn't extend to Dad; they hated each other. The husband vs. mother-in-law conflict was intensified in our family by the fact that Grandma Jessie lived with us.

When we watched movies on TV, Grandma Jessie was our commentator. She knew all the older actors back to the Gish sisters, and provided biographical information on them. About Robert Walker, she said enigmatically, "He destroyed himself." About Clark Gable, she shook her head slowly and said with enormous emphasis, "Oh, he . . . had . . . *it*." Her memories gave stature to the actors.

Sterling and I went up the childhood ladder of

viewer sophistication, from Roy Rogers to "Gun-smoke" to movies. Sterling usually identified with the lead. I equated myself with sidekicks and supporting players because they seemed more human. Sterling liked Steve McQueen because he jumped his motorcycle in *The Great Escape*. I liked McQueen because his hands got sweaty before the big gunfight in *The Magnificent Seven*. His anxiety in that situation made sense to me.

In the mid-sixties I determined that I wanted to live like Rob Petrie on "The Dick Van Dyke Show." By then our dad was getting scary, and that program soothed and encouraged me. I didn't understand all the jokes, but I could see that Rob Petrie's home was free of animosity. I thought, I want to have a house like that someday, with Mary Tyler Moore in it.

I didn't much want a house like ours, because as we got older we went through a sour period at home for about ten or fifteen years. Dad went kind of rabid. He felt confined—stuck with people he didn't like anymore. He saw himself chained for the remainder of his time to four big iron balls. He drank to be happier but instead he would get mad and decide he wanted to kill us.

As Dad became unpredictable and alarming, Sterling and I relied increasingly on TV role models. Sterling's favorite was Robert Lansing, who was probably the greatest of the television smokers.

Lansing played Frank Savage, an intense WW2 bomber squadron commander on "12 O'Clock High," and what with having to send men to their deaths over the English Channel, he went through rettes. When he took a drag during an ... ene, the smoke came out in little bursts ... the longer speeches. Sometimes he'd take a strong pull and the smoke wouldn't come out until the next episode.

Sterling modeled his smoking style on Lansing's, and I took mine from Sterling. As adults we quit, but we followed Lansing's later career with some anxiety. Since we'd used his inhalation system, we felt our survival was tied to his. It was a relief to see him continue through "The Equalizer" in the eighties and on to "Kung Fu: The Legend Continues" in the nineties.

Lansing was excellent at portraying a good boss under pressure. You could see he cared about his young fliers. Sterling preferred his method of handling people to our dad's. "If Robert Lansing was waiting in the car for the rest of the family to come out of the house," he told me once, "he wouldn't scream like Hitler in the old newsreels."

Much has been written about the enraged parent, and I don't have too much to add in reference to Dad. He was a pretty standard representative of the type. You've probably seen him dramatized, or known someone similar.

I don't want to overlook his good points. Downtown where he worked, Tall Paul Fleger was an affable string bean, with a vague look behind his glasses. He'd tell a harmless joke out of the side of his mouth. He was eager to please at the office, conscientious and sharp.

When we were little, he was fine at home too. He set up an electric train for us in the basement.

He and Mom, working separately, paid off the house in Henley and saved enough to send us to college. He took us to our first ball game and set up a badminton net in the backyard. Dad loved us; I feel sure of this.

And yet by the time we were teenagers, his most common remark to himself while walking around the house was, "Surrounded by shitheels." He said this often. If he had written a memoir, that would've been the title.

As Dad reached his late forties, he'd still be affable at work, but we weren't *at* work. At home he was bitter and ferocious.

Sterling said, "I don't know why people say accountants have no personality. Dad has two."

One time we were all in Chicago for dinner with some of Dad's colleagues. He was bouncy and bubbly with everyone at the restaurant, but as soon as we got in the car he began swearing at Mom. He took a kind of sitting swing at her in the front seat, which she ducked.

Sterling had recently seen Marlon Brando in a TV Western, and from the back seat he said, "You're a one-eyed jack in this town, Dad, but I've seen the other side of your face."

Dad nearly went nuts: "What does *that* mean? What the fuck does *that* mean?" He kept reaching back behind him to get a piece of Sterling but he couldn't because by this time we were on the Eisenhower. Dad got him when we got home, though.

I think initially Dad felt thwarted because the women in the house wouldn't let him discipline us kids as often as he wanted to. We were irritating, no doubt, Sterling and I. We made noise and broke stuff and made snotty remarks. I don't know if we were worse than most kids. We may have been. We didn't do our chores the way he wanted us to. He used to say, "Do it my way or else." Sterling always felt a need to find out what "or else" signified.

Dad made periodic strenuous attempts to cheer up and pull us all up to happiness with him. One spring evening he towed home a brand-new boat with a big Evinrude motor on the back. He had long nursed a nautical dream; he wanted to be out there on lake and river, the captain of a vessel. So on impulse, on this day, he made a down payment on this sleek suburbanite cruiser, all on his own. He seemed to expect Mom to be all happy about it. But Mom wasn't receptive to sudden large expenditures. She felt extra money should be spent on educational trips.

Dad said he'd named it the *Rita,* after her. She said he should have named it the *Selfish, Selfish, Selfish*. The result of their battle that night was a compromise: He kept the boat, but we never had a good time on it.

Mom's primary dream, I think, was to harvest greatness from the soil of a happy home. She had Sterling slated to discover a cancer cure, and I, Adlai, was expected to make up for those two Democratic losses to Ike in '52 and '56. It hurt her when the atmosphere at home turned grim; she took it as a sign that we might not make it.

The melodramatic episodes stand out in memory. Dad stuck a hatchet in the kitchen door frame over Mom's head once. Another time, he hit

Grandma Jessie and one whole side of her face turned black.

And one winter night when Mom wasn't home he dumped Grandma Jessie out into the snow in the backyard—actually threw her out of the house. Sterling came home from a date as I was helping her up, and he carried her back inside. She didn't weigh more than ninety pounds. It was frightening to hear her whimper, because she'd always been so tough.

Sterling took her upstairs and put her in bed. Dad was in the garage by then, getting a case of beer, and Sterling went out there. I followed. Dad was bent over, picking up the beer, and he had a hat on, with earflaps. Sterling took the hat off and slapped it down on Dad's head; he whapped him with it, like Curly or Larry rebelling against Moe.

Dad couldn't believe one of us had attacked him. He went wild. Sterling got behind him and they spun down the driveway together like acrobatic Russian dancers until Dad's glasses flew off. Sterling wouldn't let go because he felt safer where he was. Dad was crying, he was so frustrated; he couldn't get loose to extend himself. His teeth were clenched and he made high-pitched noises out of his nose. Neighbors came outside, and pretty soon Sterling released him. Dad chased after him but ran out of wind eventually and went panting back into the house. Sterling yelled at him, "I'm not scared of you! I'm not scared of you!" But he put a rock in his pocket before he went back inside.

Recalling Dad at moments like that may give a wrong impression. He sacrificed a lot for us. On the other hand, I'm leaving a lot of nights out.

Grandma Jessie finally moved out, to an apartment in Chicago, and died two years later. Mom quit her job to stay home with us.

There was no murder done. This turned out to be another of Dad's good points. He wanted to kill us; he told us he was going to kill us; he was mad enough and strong enough to kill us, but he never actually did it. There was a thin layer of circumspection, a membrane just over the volcano crater, that stretched nightly and leaked and got holes in it, but never entirely tore away.

One reason was that the armament for a mass impulse killing wasn't there to hand. Years later I met Dad in Chicago for lunch one day. Another office worker was sitting with us and bragging about his gun collection. Dad listened for a while, then shook his head and said mildly to me, "If I'd had a gun in the house, we'd all be dead."

I should mention that of the whole family I had it the easiest. Because I was the youngest, people were always protecting me. Sterling, Mom and Grandma Jessie deflected almost all of the anger that came my way. It mostly went over my head, which I kept down.

Sterling's reaction to our home life was defiant. He resolved to go out and become great, and then return someday in his Superman suit and force Dad's forehead to the floor.

When he turned fifteen and a half and got his learner's permit, he kidnapped Mom and drove her to the office of a female divorce lawyer he'd looked up in the Yellow Pages. Mom was touched by the gesture and even went in and consulted the lawyer. But she chose not to run, as she put it. Mom figured she was safer with Dad than trying to get away from him. She believed she could outlast him. He had his first heart attack at forty-nine.

Her decision disappointed Sterling. He worked it off by accompanying me to the local cemetery and recreating World War II, using pears from a nearby tree as grenades. We splattered the enemy tombstones and dived behind the allied tombstones. Sterling was Vic Morrow and yelled stuff like, "Kirby, get that BAR over here!" There was one tombstone that said simply, "Dade." Sterling passed by it and said gruffly, "No shit."

We grew up closer than a lot of brothers, and I believe we have Dad to thank.

CHAPTER TWO

Sterling and I goaded each other into many of the crises of our lives; I taunted him into acting.

He was tending that way anyhow. For the first two years of high school he felt invisible. As a pulling guard on the football team he enjoyed the hitting, but hated the anonymity. He would have preferred to play without a helmet so people could see who he was.

In his sophomore year he began doing personality experiments. We all try to construct an effective personality when we're teenagers. Sterling's plan was to combine in himself the distinctive characteristics of his favorite actors and become a devastating composite. He irritated me.

One slow summer evening before his junior year—this would be 1969—we were playing chess in the living room. I quit because Sterling got too Hollywood.

He walked in from the bathroom like Groucho Marx. He gestured like Peter Falk. When he took one of my pieces, he laughed like Sidney Poitier. He was a mosaic.

"Cut it out," I told him.

"Certainly, sir," he said, as Robert Culp.

"That's it," I said, rising. "I'm not playing anymore."

"Why not?"

"Because you think you're on TV, and you're not. You're just a wormy teenager playing chess with his brother."

He seemed to recognize the truth of this.

"I'm not always gonna be," he declared. "And neither are you. Someday we'll be out in Hollywood, sitting at a table just like this, only we'll be having lunch with Steve McQueen."

"Yeah," I nodded, "and we'll be saying, 'If you ever want to see your son again . . . '"

"No, he'll be asking us to be in his new movie."

Young as I was, I spotted the flaw.

"Why is he going to know who we are?" I asked. "You're screwy. You've never even been in a school play, but you call Robert Culp 'Bob,' like you know him."

"I know his work."

"It's not enough to act all around the house, Ster. You gotta do it in an auditorium."

He gazed at me thoughtfully, deciding whether to beat me up. I looked down at the chessboard.

"It took nerve for you to say that," he said

finally. Then he gave me a friendly punch on the point of the shoulder. His fist felt like a cinder block.

That fall he auditioned for a play at Henley High—*Mrs. McThing,* by Mary Chase. Sterling considered the material beneath him. He was primarily influenced at this time by TV viewings of *Night and the City,* with Richard Widmark, and *Vera Cruz,* with Burt Lancaster. But he was proud to get a part on his first try. He played Virgil, the singing waiter, a minor role with comic business.

Mom and I were first-nighters. Mom was excited. She had always encouraged us to be artistic. When she was young, she took a writing course from Thornton Wilder, and she had read us bedtime stories expressively. At her work at the doctor's office, she typed speedily without looking at her fingers and was altogether professional—even grim. But at home, with other adults visiting, she was girlish and giggly, and tried to act out funny stories she'd heard at work. She would laugh giddily and get lost during the setup, digressing while everyone waited, exasperated, for the punch line. "*Anyway,*" she would say somewhere in the middle, and meander on. I don't think she ever got a joke right.

On this night she was proud; Sterling got his laughs. When he was on, you watched him even if there were ten other people onstage. This was partly because, as a waiter, he was moving.

After that he was in *Come Back, Little Sheba.* He was truly good in that.

I can speak with authority because most Midwesterners know acting. You probably do too.

We've seen so much of it on TV during the winters. Thanks to Grandma Jessie I'm above average in my ability to assess talent; I have often spotted star quality.

In *Come Back, Little Sheba* Sterling played a middle-aged alcoholic. He was only sixteen, so he kind of went in and out of the guy's age. But he stunned everyone anyway, including me. I was expecting to see him up there as three parts Earl Holliman to two parts Warren Oates or somebody, so I wasn't prepared for what he did.

He was subdued and mild at the beginning, but when he fell off the wagon he got spooky. He wasn't a drunk like another kid might do, slurring his words. You could understand him easily, just like we always understood Dad. He worked himself up like Dad. And when he got the knife from the kitchen cabinet and began terrorizing his wife, he was even *better* than Dad.

Then later, when he came back from the dry-out ward and he was remorseful, he moved so carefully and delicately, Mom had to get up and leave. It upset her to watch.

You could tell he had it.

Sterling became an actor halfway through high school, which separated us considerably. I was a freshman when he was a junior, so my arrival as a nobody coincided with his as a somebody. Now he had girls calling him up. I couldn't even get them to come to the phone.

During my freshman year I fell in love with Sharon Landis, a dazzling blonde in my French class who was a cheerleader and, just to ram home how hopeless it was, a senior. My yearning for her had a large component of romantic sappiness. I thought she was radiant walking through snow in a cap. It was easier to imagine lunch with Steve McQueen than to imagine a world in which Sharon Landis and I were a couple. But I went to sleep most nights that year trying to dream one up.

She lived on the other side of DuPage Road. Her house was at the foot of a hill, on a sun-dappled block of colonial homes. I would ride my bike down the hill, past her house, like Tom Sawyer showing off for Becky Thatcher. Now I guess it would be called stalking.

I was coasting down her street one day when she came around the corner and nearly ran me down in her convertible. Sterling was seated next to her in the front seat. They were returning from playing tennis. He was surprised to see me in that neighborhood. The contrast between that car and my bike was vast and humiliating.

I couldn't stand the sight of Sterling for a few weeks after that, and when he finally became aware of it he decided to advise me about women. He told me to become an actor, like him.

"Listen to me, I'll never tell you anything more important: Girls love stars."

The two of us were in the kitchen, and he paused, chewing toast, to let this sink in. "Sports, music, theater, doesn't matter. Girls all talked and looked right past me, right over my shoulder until I started acting, and now—look." He reached into a notebook and flashed a poem Joyce Riddle had written him. Joyce Riddle was a junior, a stunning redhead, so tall that I didn't even bother fantasizing about her. I stared at the paper avidly. What I saw seemed very pro-Sterling, but he pulled it away before any of it could sink in except the phrase "deep eyes."

"See, now I'm deep," he said. "Before, I was '*Ster*ling? *Euuu*wwww.' It's the spotlight. It hypnotizes 'em. They're like rabbits in the road." He brooded darkly, holding the poem. "God forbid they should love you for yourself."

I was impressed, but I knew he was making it sound too easy.

"Don't you get nervous up there in front of everybody?"

He shook his head, then corrected the shake. "Well, yes. At the start of the opening performance. That's pretty bad. Your heartbeat really zooms. But get past the first line or two and you're okay. And you'll be good, don't worry. Adoptees make the best actors, because we aren't shackled by ethnic thinking. We can be everybody. Or at least, I'm gonna be."

So I tried it, once, as a sophomore. But I learned that I would have to get my girls another way.

The play was *Arsenic and Old Lace,* another old-time farce. I auditioned with Sterling and was cast—everyone who auditioned was cast—but it soon became clear that Ernest Borgnine had nothing to fear from me.

Sterling was the lead, Mortimer Brewster. I had a small role as Lt. Rooney, one of the cops. Sterling was good as a character who thinks he'll go crazy because insanity runs in his family; he finally finds out he isn't really a "Brewster" after all.

But as Lt. Rooney, I was flat. When I was on, the audience coughed. I coughed myself. I had a scene with Sterling in Act III, when one of my speeches led up to a knock on the door. I couldn't remember this speech, so nobody knocked on the door. We just stood there on stage and got older.

I finally said, "You want to start over, Ster?"

Sterling seemed to expand in his costume. His eyes bulged. Then he said, "I hear somebody on the porch."

Afterward he was gentle with me because he thought I might be suicidal. "If you're gonna go on in theater," he said, "here's a tip: Don't call the actors by their given names during a performance."

When I told him I didn't think acting was for me, he got sore and said, "Well, what is?"

My lack of drive frustrated the family. I just didn't know what I wanted to do. I thought I might like to be a submarine commander, but I didn't want to be in the military. Mom had had me take piano for four years but I showed little talent; my left hand, Dad noted, was even lazier than the rest of me.

If I could interject a question here: Was my birth father, when young, easily fatigued—like one of those characters on "Hee Haw" who used to lie out in front of the shack all day? Or were you? I'm not trying to evade responsibility. It's just that I used to wonder whether I was congenitally inert or just did it on my own.

Anyway . . . there was no fire in my belly, or even kindling. I picked my way through high school without distinction. Mom said I was a dreamer, but I didn't dream about anything in particular. I liked quiet, because quiet was rare. At home Dad still spoke as if we were all stuck to his shoe.

In 1971 Sterling left for Buchanan College downstate. Right up to the end, Dad was telling him he wouldn't live to go.

Sterling came back for vacations for a year or two, and Mom and I visited him twice. He became a big actor on campus almost immediately. Every time I saw him, he had a different girlfriend. I remember Susie, Anita, Gail, Marcia and Lee Ann. Most of them were in the theater department, and I liked all of them except Lee Ann.

She intimidated me. She was tall and skinny, with stringy hair and disdainful eyes. Unlike Sterling's other girlfriends, she was a sociology major. She woke him up to what was going on in the world.

She wasn't good-looking in an immediately apparent way, but she was so intense that you kept looking at her out of the corner of your eye to see how she was reacting to things. She came home with Sterling for Easter break one year. She wore a pea coat. She showed contempt better and more often than anyone I'd ever met.

Sterling, who had filled out to grown-up linebacker size by then, seemed hypnotized by her activism. She had him wearing a poncho. He had told her he was "apolitical," and she had replied, "Then you're a-alive." She told him that a lot of the things he liked were bullshit. Many of his favorite Hollywood films, and *all* of his old TV shows, were bullshit. So were the well-made plays of his high school days. Lee Ann felt that radicalized theater was the only kind with any value.

She had a snort-laugh she used to convey disdain. She called Sterling "Wally," for Wally Cleaver, and I knew what that made me—Beaver Fleger. She looked at Mom, Dad and me dispassionately, expecting nothing. We amused her because we were so middle class. She was suburban herself, but she had repudiated her background. Dad was taken aback by her and showed her no hostility at all; I think he sensed that she was giving Sterling a hard time.

She was right about Sterling's lack of depth. He'd started acting so he could be somebody else, have fun, get girls and show Dad. He could perform powerfully on a small-scale, personal level, but he had no theory. He saw no big picture. Now he was faced with the extermination of the Indians, pollution, oppression of blacks and women, Vietnam and the military-industrial complex. This was mostly due to Lee Ann, and it was painful.

"She says I'm prostituting myself and I haven't even made any money yet," he confided to me as we drank beer in the basement one night. "I'm not even supposed to do Neil Simon."

"How much do you like her?"

He thought about it. "She's got more to her than the actresses I know. And sexually, she's . . . inventive."

Well, I thought *that* was living. They did LSD

together too. One evening earlier in that vacation they went out together for what Sterling called "an electric walk." They didn't come back until three in the morning and Sterling said the only places they went were the train station and the lawn in front of City Hall.

They broke up the next year, though, 1973 or '74, following an argument over the movie *The Way We Were*. "She called me a dumbass for the thousandth time," Sterling would say later.

On this night in the basement, Sterling was concerned about me. We were surrounded by family relics: a wooden ramp Dad once made for us to race toy cars on . . . a dismantled electric train . . . barbecue paraphernalia—each item a memory of some long-ago blowup. That fall I was to attend Duquesne Junior College, close to Henley. It was less expensive than Buchanan—more in keeping with my scholastic achievements. I was supposed to live at home for at least another year. Dad didn't want me to have the access to college women that Sterling had had. The sexual revolution had contributed to Dad's bitterness. He felt he'd been born too soon.

"What are *you* gonna do?" Sterling asked me on this night. He meant a career.

I looked around the basement.

"You're gonna have to do something," he said.

"Mounted policeman," I said.

"Don't you have a feeling inside that points you one direction or another?"

Odd that he should have said that. One morning when I was about twelve, looking out the kitchen window, I suddenly suffered a melancholy longing I could feel in my chest. Grandma Jessie saw me staring out the window at the squirrel in the bird feeder and asked what was the matter. I said, "I want something, but I don't know what I want." It wasn't food, it wasn't a bike. It wasn't the squirrel. It wasn't love from my family; I knew they loved me. It wasn't anything else I could name. But it hurt.

On this night I told Sterling, "Don't worry about me." Then I added, "How do you mean, she's 'inventive'?"

He sighed, and gave up on me.

CHAPTER THREE

I had no real expectations for myself. I think I pictured life as a deal where other people would do stuff and A. J. Fleger would comment on it. The only goal I had in my teens, apart from some shabby ambitions regarding girls, was getting out of the house intact. Beyond that, I didn't see myself amounting to much. It was Sterling whom I pictured up in the sky someday. I assumed he would eventually become a shining star.

Instead, in March of 1975, he became a bottle rocket.

In his senior year at Buchanan he performed in an improvisational sketch comedy group with five other students. They appeared at other colleges around the state, and Mom and I saw them when they played the University of Chicago. They did a ninety-minute show with about twenty bits in it,

Second City style. Sterling was funny as a college professor analyzing the lyrics to the Beatles song "Birthday," and as a pitchman for a knife company, Camino Cutlery ("Remember, ladies—the way to a man's heart is through his chest"). He said afterward that he was scared, but I didn't see it.

They sent a videotape of that show as a demo to New York, to Michael Adderley, the producer of the new "Manhattan Live" program. Eventually, back came an invitation for the "professor" who did the Beatles sketch to come out there for an interview. Sterling discussed the invitation with the rest of the group and they urged him to go so he could get them jobs later when he got famous. He dropped his course work and went.

Dad said $60,000 in tuition was turning to sewage. Mom took it better. She admired Sterling for seizing the day.

A few nights after Sterling left Buchanan, he called us from the Big Time. They had auditioned him and signed him for small parts in two sketches to be performed live, as they all were on that show, on an upcoming Friday night.

"Where are you sleeping?" asked Mom on the upstairs extension.

"I'm staying at a girl's apartment in Brooklyn named Shirley," he said. "She works on the crew. She's really nice."

He said the parts weren't big enough to merit Mom's coming out to sit in the audience, but she asked me to go to lend moral support, and I gladly went. I had been reading about existentialism at Duquesne and had taken it to mean that it didn't matter if I attended classes or not. So I was in New York the following Wednesday, with my eyeballs out to here.

They did "Manhattan Live" on the thirty-ninth floor of a skyscraper, on a small stage surrounded by cables, cameras and lights. Sterling got me in to see a blocking rehearsal where I met the regular cast. Well, I saw them. They were all young, not famous yet, pretty clubby and tense. It was a live national show and they didn't have a lot of time to prepare. I knocked over an offstage ashtray once and they all turned and looked at me as if . . . Well, I guess I was.

The women in the cast were skinny and dynamic. I liked Judee Consolo best because she laughed at what other people did. Joel Donlin and Art Klee were the male stars. Donlin was slight and slouchy; Klee was heavyset. They mostly just talked to each other and Michael Adderley, who oversaw everything.

Sterling had one speaking part, as a cop in a lineup routine. He had lines like "Number one, step forward." He stood with his back to the house, so he couldn't make much of an impression. During the runthrough he asked Adderley if he should use an accent. Before Adderley could answer, Art Klee said, "You want a peg leg too?"

Sterling was more prominent in a bit based on the public's fascination with Charles Manson and the upcoming TV movie *Helter Skelter*. Its premise had Manson appearing as the mystery celebrity guest on the old "What's My Line?" TV game show. It was staged just as that program had been, with one addition. When Manson (played by Joel Donlin) came onstage to sign his name on the blackboard, Sterling and a blond girl followed him and stood behind him as he sat with the moderator. Across the stage, four blindfolded panelists tried to identify the guest by asking yes-or-no questions.

In Thursday rehearsals they did it just like "What's My Line?" except that every time one of the panelists asked a question that got a "No" answer, Manson's followers went over and stabbed the panelist to death. (The John Daley moderator character said, "That's one down and three to go to you, Arlene," and so on.) Finally, Judee Consolo as Peggy Cass, the fourth blindfolded panelist and lone survivor, asked for a "conference" with her colleagues. Feeling the corpses slumped next to her, she slowly realized that the guest must be "Charlie Manson!" Then Michael Adderley called out "Applause-applause-applause" and Joel Donlin, as Manson, crossed the stage, shook hands with Judee, waved at the audience and exited with his followers as the three dead panelists slumped to the floor.

Kind of black, you might say. But Michael Adderley said it had a satirical point, about killers as cover boys, and he assured everyone it would go over. Dave LeBaron, the actor playing panelist Bennett Cerf, didn't agree.

"I didn't like it yesterday and I don't like it today," he said.

"Dave," said Adderley from the lip of the stage, "when Joel comes out and signs Manson's name on that blackboard, we're gonna get the biggest laugh of the night."

"It's bad taste," LeBaron said.

"Bad taste," said Art Klee, who played the moderator, John Charles Daley, "is when you do the news and we hear crickets."

"I don't like it," said LeBaron.

"Thank you, Dave," said Adderley. "You're on record."

Sterling did his follower part like a zombie, which was correct, I thought.

He and his new girlfriend Shirl took me out the night before the show. We went to a restaurant/bar somewhere in Manhattan, I don't remember the name of it. It was bright lights outside and in. Everybody was young and animated. Band in the bar. Sterling talked three times as fast as he used to. I was agog about everything, but I acted calm in front of Shirl.

She was a short, tired-looking, dark-haired girl with a nice figure. She had snapped up Sterling right out of his audition.

"They're really straightforward out here, A.J.," said Sterling when she went to the ladies' room. "The women who work in theater especially. They're hungry for heterosexual males."

"They *tell* you this?" I asked.

"Shirl did."

I looked around the bar, but none of the girls looked back. They all seemed satisfied with whoever they were with.

"She's kind of on the rebound, though," Sterling shouted, over the music.

"Who from?"

"Well, the rest of the cast."

"You nervous about tomorrow?" I asked.

Sterling bobbed his head up and down about twenty times.

"Under control, though," he bellowed. "I don't have to say anything except 'Step forward.' "

He leaned toward me and spoke more softly.

"I can do this. I'm as good as these guys. It won't show right away, but you'll see. You're gonna be proud of me."

He grinned at me. He looked about twelve. I was touched. I hadn't known he cared about my opinion.

"Good," I called back. "Listen. Can I get a job on this crew with the straightforward girls?"

I slept in the living room in Shirl's Brooklyn apartment that night, and we all got up at seven Friday morning, the day of the show. Sterling's right eye was bloodshot, so he sat in the living room with his eyes closed while Shirl got dressed. He thought the eye would clear sooner if he kept it shut.

Shirl had a little tabby cat named Rikki, maybe six months old, who was always skulking and pouncing around. As I sat on the couch and Sterling dozed in the chair by the window in his underwear, Rikki came into the living room, on patrol. As she approached us, she noticed some threat or invader high up on the wall, and decided she had to leap up to the window curtain. In order to do that, she had to run up Sterling's chest and face, which she did.

He shot up screaming out of the chair, swinging at air. Rikki soared into the curtains and ricocheted onto the floor.

Sterling stood in the middle of the room while

the claw marks bloomed on his face. They were quite noticeable on either side of his eyes, and there was a deep gouge over one eyebrow where the cat had pushed off. Aside from the cosmetic damage, it had to be painful.

Shirl came in while he advanced on the cat. He grabbed Rikki off the floor and held her up in his right hand to spike her.

"*Hey!*" said Shirl.

"Yyyyyy*ahh!*" said Sterling, but he mastered himself at the last second and kind of shot-put Rikki onto the couch. Then he spun in agony, his hands to his eyes, as Oedipus might do. "Your cat ran up my *face.*"

"Well, she didn't mean it."

"Up my *face*—the *show* is tonight."

He strode to a wall mirror and examined himself.

"Well, this is swell," he said. "I look like I was in a fork fight."

"Can't they cover it up?" I asked.

"Yeah, with *gauze.* Look at this, it's *spreading.* Well, they won't use me, that's all. Why would they use me? I'm a tick-tack-toe face. Y'know, I thought I might blow my line or have a heart attack, but I never— Lemme ask you something, kitty." He stalked back across the room and grabbed the window curtain. "What was so important up here? Hmm?" He ripped the curtain off the wall and brandished the cloth. "Show me."

The cat cleaned herself.

"Kittens are like that," said Shirl.

•　　•　　•

Sterling sat bleakly between Shirl and me in the subway going downtown. At one stop he turned to me and asked, "Is it better or worse?"

"Darker," I said.

But Michael Adderley didn't flinch or recoil from Sterling's face. Instead he made a Napoleonic adjustment. He let him keep his role as the lineup cop since Sterling had his back to the audience in that one anyway, and in the Manson sketch, Adderley used the accident to move him up in importance. He gave him Dave LeBaron's two-line part as Bennett Cerf, since the blindfold would cover the cuts. LeBaron got *his* wish, which was to get out of the bit altogether, and Sterling was replaced in his original nonspeaking zombie stabber part by the scraggliest extra on the crew.

Sterling did his new role barefaced in rehearsal, because the blindfolds weren't ready. He said his two new lines perfectly. Afterward he seemed stunned by his good fortune. Shirl told him, "You owe Rikki some raw liver."

Before joining the audience that night, I approached him backstage to offer encouragement. He was yawning and shooting his elbows back behind him rhythmically. He said he felt all right except for his bladder and his lungs.

"I've forgotten how to breathe," he said matter-of-factly. "I take it in but I don't convert it. The only way I can get any oxygen is if I yawn."

Actually he looked ready—pumped, but not panicky. Whenever he really needed to breathe, he did push-ups.

"Think Dad'll watch?" he asked.

I said sure, Dad and Mom both.

Then something occurred to me and I blurted it. I probably shouldn't have said it. I certainly shouldn't have said it *then*.

"Hey, you know what? This is the first time in your life that *both* dads and *both* moms might watch."

He stared at me blankly, blinking. Then he walked away without another word.

"Break a leg," I called after him.

Funny that I should have thought of that remark about the dads and moms. We hardly ever talked about being adopted anymore, or thought about it either. I don't believe it had surfaced in my head in the last year. But that night it struck me as a diverting sidelight to Sterling's TV debut. So out it came.

The studio crowd was young, rowdy and keyed up. They whooped and looked for themselves on the monitors when a camera panned the seats. I hoped they were all as high as they acted, because they figured to laugh more that way. Behind my fourth-row seat, a guy about my age introduced himself to the girl seated next to him in a conversation that was fairly typical of the era. He said his last name was Dray.

"Gray?" she asked.

"No, Dray."

"Gray?"

"No, Dray."

"Bray?"

"No, *Dray*," the guy said, exasperated and disgusted with her by now. "*D,* as in '*Dope.*'"

"Oh," said the girl. "Well. Right on."

I was nervous myself, but expectant. I thought it would be the first step on a golden road for Sterling. I remember feeling a slight trace of sand in my collar about how smoothly things were going for him. Send 'em a tape and you're on TV. Cat scratches you, you get a bigger part. God seemed to be tweaking all the obstructions out of his path. But basically I was happy for him. And I had hopes of ending up on the crew.

The Manson bit opened the show; they did it even before the theme and credits. I thought this was good, because it didn't give Sterling time to hang around backstage and worry. Also it meant the crowd was at its most responsive, not having had to sit through any clinkers.

The lights came up on the "What's My Line?" set, with Art Klee as John Daley, seated on the right.

Downstage on the left sat Sterling, with that prominent jawline, as Bennett Cerf. His fellow panelists were angled upstage toward center. Sterling's right profile was to cameras and audience. You couldn't see the cat scratches under the big black blindfold, which was snug around his eyes. His head was up as he listened to John Daley's introduction of the mystery guest.

When Joel Donlin entered in a long-haired wig and signed Charles Manson's name on the blackboard, the studio crowd went crazy. Adderley had been right. They howled. I thought, This is something. People are going to talk about this. Sterling can always say his debut was in the Charles Manson sketch on "Manhattan Live."

Of the panelists, he was first—first to talk, first to be killed. As he began his opening line, he scared me by coughing. (He told me later that his heart had skipped a beat and that caused the cough.) Then, recovering, he said, "Thank you, John. I'd like to ask our mystery guest, Are you connected with show business?"

Perfect. Manson, assuming a French accent, leaned forward in his seat and murmured, "Oui." That was a nice touch, I thought; the celebrity mystery guests used to disguise their voices on "What's My Line?" The audience was falling in with the whole idea. It was going great.

Now Sterling had his other line. He was *supposed* to say, "I'm going to act on a sudden hunch here . . . Are you . . . Charles Boyer?"

Then Klee, as Daley, was to say, "No. That's one down and three to you, Arlene," while Manson's followers crossed the stage and stabbed Sterling.

Instead of which . . .

Instead of which, Sterling cocked his head as though thinking deeply and said, "I'm going to act on a sudden hunch here . . . Are you . . . Charles Manson?"

You see the difference.

I don't know how familiar you are with sketch humor. One thing about it is that it's dependent on the proper construction, like a house. You put the roof on before you've put up the walls and that roof is going to proceed full speed straight down to the ground.

Sterling didn't really have to say "Charles

Boyer" for the bit to work. He could have said Charles Aznavour, Charles De Gaulle, Charles Lindbergh, or he could've left *out* Charles and said Lyle Talbot or Clu Gulager or Micklebar Nelson, any name really, and safely gotten his "No" answer and his stabbing and it would have gone on all right. But when he said, "Are you Charles Manson?" he strangled the concept.

I couldn't tell if he realized what he'd said. The panelist on his left quivered a bit. Sterling's visible face, below the blindfold, was frozen in an expectant smile. There was a pause, lasting the better part of the evening.

The audience was confused. A tentative laugh died out. Klee and Donlin were chewing over how to respond to "Are you Charles Manson?" If Donlin, as Manson, said, "No," the rest of the bit would be senseless. If he said, "Yes," it would be over.

All Klee, as John Daley, could finally think of to say after Sterling's catastrophic flub was "No, he is not Dolley Madison." Pretty weak, I know, but I've had years to think about it and haven't come up with anything better. I personally would have used my old "Want to start over?" line.

Anyway, Klee said what he said, and the Manson followers crossed the stage; Sterling was stabbed, with extra emphasis, I thought, and died . . . again.

The bit went on, but it never recovered. The audience couldn't figure out that Manson-Madison exchange. After the blackout I didn't see Sterling onstage again. When the lineup sketch came on later, there was somebody else up there whose back I didn't recognize.

After the show I was allowed backstage in time to see Art Klee go after Sterling.

The male actors were in a little locker room, changing into their street clothes. Sterling was already in his, sitting on a small bench. Klee was standing, sweating through his last costume, a pirate outfit, saying, "I want to know where Mike got this guy."

"Forget it," said Dave LeBaron.

"No-no-no," said Klee. "You weren't out there. You begged off. I was the one with the bucket of shit on his head. Right?" He spoke to Sterling, who sat with his head down.

Michael Adderley walked in and Klee turned to address him:

"Your guy Needledick here wet his pants and killed the one decent bit of the night, made us look like fucking fools."

Sterling just sat there.

"Tell you something, Strongheart," Klee continued, leaning over Sterling and speaking softly and hoarsely down into his ear. "You should sing in the shower. You should jack off in bed. You should act in the mirror. But you shouldn't do anything that involves other people. Pull your own if you can find it, but don't bring it around here."

"Artie, talk to *me*," Adderley said. But he didn't say anything to Sterling. Neither did Donlin or LeBaron or anybody else.

"Guy killed me out there," Klee said. "You know, I don't put up with that."

"Everybody's blown lines," said Adderley.

"Not like that! He said the one thing to fuck up the whole bit! How many lines did he have, anyway, two?"

"You want to shut up?" I said.

Klee looked at me blankly.

"Say again?"

"My brother," said Sterling.

"Oh." Klee leaned toward me, inquisitive. "What do *you* do, pee on your leg?"

I launched myself forward and got in a glancing blow to his head before Sterling came roaring up from his bench and got between us.

"Back *off*," said Sterling fiercely, pushing me until I hollered at him.

"What are you taking it for? I'd *bite* anybody talked to me like that."

"Well, he wasn't talking to you, was he?"

"So you said the wrong line, you made a mis—"

"Shut up. Come on. Don't make me kill ya."

He pushed me back out toward the door.

"Don't forget to wash your pants," said Klee from behind him.

Sterling muttered, "Okay," turned, walked back two steps and straight-armed Klee in the forehead with the heel of his palm. Klee fell over one of the little benches and ended up sitting against a locker with his feet in the air, staring marble-eyed at his shoes.

I elbowed past Sterling, looked down at Klee and said, "It's easy to criticize"—another weak line that would have benefited from preparation time.

We left the building, escorted by security

people. Nobody followed with an invitation to go out and party with the cast and crew.

I kept up with Sterling for a while on the street, but he finally started choking me and wouldn't stop until I promised I'd leave him alone. I went back to Shirl's place, but she came home with a different guy and I felt awkward. Sterling never showed up. I went out to the airport first thing in the morning.

And that was Sterling's career on "Manhattan Live." Michael Adderley didn't offer any more roles, and Sterling didn't ask for any. He and Shirl broke up without having to mention it to each other.

You might say, Well, it was only one word. It was only one scene. It was just one of life's embarrassing moments. And he was wearing a blindfold, after all. Nobody even knew who he was.

I said all those things to him that night, afterward. But it didn't count for anything. In his view, he had had his chance, and he had choked, and that was that. In order to stand up to the derision of your peers, you have to disagree with their opinion. Sterling didn't. He thought Art Klee was right.

Sometimes, before that Friday night, he used to have the actor's nightmare. He'd told me about it. In it, he would arrive backstage in a theater to find he was about to open in a play, usually something tricky like Shakespeare, without having been to rehearsals or learning any of the lines. I guess it's the performer's fundamental anxiety dream. But after "Manhattan Live," he no longer had it. From then on, whenever his sleeping mind wanted to horrify him, it just flipped back to that night in New York and he dreamed that.

I flew back to Chicago knowing I'd distracted him with that backstage remark about the moms and the dads. I've felt bad about it ever since. It was like I whacked his elbow while he was signing his name.

CHAPTER FOUR

Here's something I read not long ago. James Baldwin wrote it: "The young think that failure is the Siberian end of the line, banishment from all the living."

I don't know if Sterling ever saw that sentiment, but he fell in with it. After "Manhattan Live," we didn't see him for quite a while. Instead of returning to college, he went to work on a farm in Virginia. Later he moved to the West Coast and wound up as a job counselor for an employment agency. He seemed to prefer the company of people he hadn't known previously. Mom never entirely got over his failure to go back and graduate from Buchanan. They eventually reconciled, but the relationship was altered to Mother and Disappointment.

As for me, at twenty I informed Mom and Dad

of the flaws I'd detected in their parenting and moved into Chicago, where I spent the next decade and a half changing apartments. I loved the city and staying up late, but I can't say I had a plan. To show my superiority to Dad, I drank like a gentleman for twelve years.

In Alcoholics Anonymous, of which I eventually became a member, they say you stop growing while you're drinking; you freeze. However old you are when you start, that's the age you are emotionally when you stop. So I stayed twenty from 1976 to 1988. I was a friendly drunk, sort of sentimental. I'd sing.

If I noticed a defect in my character, I assigned its origin to Dad or Mom, or you or blood Dad, or a combination. I had a couple bouts of curiosity about you. One day, at a girlfriend's suggestion, I charged over to the DuPage County courthouse with a medium buzz on and demanded to see my birth records. I was told they were sealed, so I charged back to Chicago again.

I didn't work toward anything, beyond payday. In retrospect, if I had to limit myself to one piece of advice to young people, I would say: make your dream specific. Otherwise you'll end up working a stamping machine, trying to sell encyclopedias, bartending at Mona's and scraping paint. None of these jobs is disgraceful, but when you say that for them, you've told the tale.

I hated scraping paint the most, but at least I could do it. Selling encyclopedias was impossible. Didn't matter where I was: Joliet, Elgin, Aurora, Naperville. They didn't want to hear my speech.

I carried a clipboard door to door because I was supposed to be taking a survey. Only later was I to reveal Volumes I and II in a hidden briefcase. But the customers had seen my kind before. One huge man of the house listened to my opening sentence and asked, "Are you selling encyclopedias?"

"No," I replied promptly.

"Because if you are," he said quietly, "I won't pay the money for the books. But I'll gladly pay that much to track your ass down."

After closing their doors on me, people would call their neighbors to warn them I was coming. I took to skipping houses in the afternoons, going only to the ones I thought were unoccupied. I liked the ones with porch swings. I'd sit on the swings and pretend I lived there.

I really believed in those encyclopedias, but I couldn't communicate my enthusiasm. The experience made me appreciate the tenacity and endurance of salespeople. After I was fired I told myself that if I ever again got the opportunity to sell a product I believed in, I'd change my approach. I'd write the speech and send somebody else out to deliver it.

My relationships with women during this time lasted about as long as my jobs—one day to three years. Women tended to like me at first for being easygoing and then, later on, not to.

All I can say in mitigation for all the things I didn't do is that I hadn't found my goal. Nothing occurred to me to make me say "Eureka." I knew there was something missing, but I wasn't unhappy; it was just that I was more interested in stuff like the Cubs and Bears than I was in my own life. There was no real sense of urgency, or time passing. You could tell I'd been the baby of the family.

In 1983 Dad had a third heart attack and died, and Sterling came back to Henley for the funeral. I thought he might appear greatly aged from the trauma of his "Manhattan Live" experience, but he didn't seem to have changed much. The jaw still stuck out. He was well dressed. His face was tanned; the last time I'd seen him it had been blotchy. He looked fine.

So did Dad. Sterling and I stood over the coffin together at the viewing the night before the service. They'd done a great job on Tall Paul. He seemed robust in his dark blue suit.

Sterling said, "He looks like he could sit right up and say 'You betcha.' "

In his last years Dad had mellowed slightly, or anyway he had slept more. But his heart had been irreparably damaged by previous rages. Looking down at him, I remembered being little, when he was okay. I would wait on our corner while the train pulled in at the Burlington depot two blocks down. I used to pick him out from the other men a block away, then watch him get bigger as he approached. When he got to me, he'd take my hand and our connected shadows would lengthen as we walked back to the house.

He hadn't killed us, after all. He'd loaned me money twice after I left home, money I hadn't yet paid back.

Mom stood erect, off to the side, grooves in her

face. She must have remembered a younger man also, because she cried a bit.

"I swore I'd never marry a man who drank," she said later. "I think whatever you say at eighteen, you are guaranteed to live to contradict."

After she went to bed that night, Sterling and I sat in the kitchen and drank beer and caught up. At that time I worked as a deckhand on the Valhalla boat rides on the Chicago River, and he said, "That sounds fun."

I was mildly surprised to hear that he and Lee Ann, his college girlfriend, had gotten back together. They had met again in Southern California, where she was working on her Master's.

"It's on violence in the movies," he told me. "She's tabulating every gunshot fired in an American film since talkies came in."

"Isn't that kind of like picking nits out of the rug?"

"Yeah, well," said Sterling, "she picked *me* out of the rug a while back. I owe her. And she's right about the movies. They aren't just movies, they have an effect."

He sipped his beer.

"But for a day-to-day relationship, it's not enough just to be right. You have to be sane."

He didn't elaborate, so I asked him what he was doing.

"I'm still at Dittmer's," he said.

As a counselor at Dittmer's Employment Resources, he coached clients on how to interview for jobs.

"I videotape them," he said. "Teach them how to sit and talk. Henry Higgins."

He winced slightly at a "Manhattan Live" promo on the little black-and-white set Mom kept in the kitchen, so I changed channels, but I got a Joel Donlin–Art Klee movie. Sterling laughed.

"I used to wish that show would get canceled and everybody on it would just die. And here the goddamn thing's still running and half of 'em are movie stars. Good thing I'm not sensitive."

I asked if he was doing any acting, and he snorted.

"Y'know what Brando says about acting—'It's the expression of a neurotic impulse. Quitting acting, that's the sign of maturity.' Think Mom'll be okay here?"

"She loves the house."

We sat for a bit. It was peaceful. Sterling looked at the scar on the pantry door frame where Dad had swung his mighty axe one night and stuck it in the wood over Mom's head.

"I thought Dad behaved very well today," he said finally.

I nodded. We sipped our beer.

"No more one-eyed jack," I said.

"Nope," said Sterling deliberately. "Now he's a dead-eyed dick."

"Dade," I said.

"No shit."

Mom yelled downstairs to ask what we were giggling about. "Your father loved you very much, you know," she called.

Well, and he did.

• • •

Now if you freeze that scene for a moment and focus in on the older brother, what do you see? Any lingering effects from that experience on TV eight years before? Maybe a trace, but no more. That face has adjusted to lowered expectations. The man in that frame has made his peace, and he's making his pile. I worry more about the younger brother, lodged in the corner behind the Bud cans—the one who looks like Tony Orlando in that suit.

But five years later, on September 13, 1988, I finally sobered up. I'm very proud of this. It was the first accomplishment of my life. I give myself credit even though I couldn't do it by myself and had to go to AA. It changes your whole outlook when you manage to do something difficult.

Then in January 1990 I got a long-distance call from a stranger named Toni Boyce, asking me to come out to California and see Sterling because she didn't know who else could help him.

"I know *I* can't," she said.

"Who are you?" I asked.

"I'm a friend, and I work with Sterling, and I care about him very much, we all do . . . and we wish he was happier."

"Why isn't he?"

"We're not sure. But I know he cares about you, and he says he's invited you out here before, but you've never come. And I kind of think you should."

"What's wrong with him? I talked to him not too long ago and he sounded okay."

"I think you should see him for yourself. Pretty soon."

She offered no details, and when I called Sterling, he sounded fine. But I invited myself out for a visit anyway.

I was ready for a change. I'd been in Chicago so long that it was stale, and I was more at fault than the town. My last girlfriend, a waitress, had said that she could fall asleep more easily with me than any man she'd known. I tried to take it as a compliment but I couldn't. They say the sons often grow up to become like the fathers. I'd resisted that, but in doing so I'd become a kind of sedative.

I wasn't worried about leaving Mom on her own. She was warm and dry at home in Henley, walking through the house at her own pace—the winner. She had friends who didn't mind dropping by now that Dad was gone. Sometimes she'd reminisce, following a good memory with a bad, veering back and forth and finally saying, "Oh, the hell with it."

Sterling seemed all right when he met me at John Wayne Airport in Orange County on a late January evening. Of course, he had a lot of talent, so I couldn't tell for sure.

Our lack of resemblance had intensified. He was tan and California fit, with sunglasses, slightly receding curly hair and his chin jutting forward more than ever. With a little early touch of gray, he looked like a Rolls-Royce. I was pale. I have a central European look, as you may recall. You could tell which of us was from out of town.

He hauled my bags out to his Lexus and drove us to an apartment complex in Irvine, an upscale, sprawled-out community about forty-five minutes south of Los Angeles. In California they always gauge distance by driving time. He had a second-floor apartment with a balcony overlooking a swimming pool.

We were greeted there by Toni Boyce, who was pretty and bird-boned, with dark hair and big, bright, panicky eyes. She didn't refer to our phone conversation. Sterling introduced her as his friend from work. There was no evidence of Lee Ann anywhere in the four rooms, so I assumed that once again she and Sterling had pffft. I wondered for a second if he'd killed her.

It was a pretty night, so we sat out on the little balcony. The pool was all lit up, a radiant turquoise rectangle. We were above and set back from the deep end, where a muscular guy and a muscular girl were diving in and climbing out, diving in and climbing out. It was like the Holiday Inn.

"I took the day off in honor of your arrival," said Sterling, "and went to Santa Anita. Got four in the Pick Six."

"Is that good?" I asked.

"Not quite, no," he said. "But I saw Elisha Cook, Jr., going up the escalator to the clubhouse."

"Get out."

"Who's he?" asked Toni. Sterling sighed.

"He was Icepick in 'Magnum,'" I said.

"Hell with that," said Sterling. "He was in *The Maltese Falcon.* 'The cheaper the crook, the gaudier the patter.' And nobody noticed him today but me and the clubhouse guard. Jack Palance killed him in *Shane*. He got killed in everything. He's walking history."

"Did you say hi?"

"Nah. We're not on the same, y'know. If I saved him from drowning or something, but . . . you and I, we'll go to Santa Anita. Racing's great. It's got nothing to do with anything."

He explained that breeding was important in thoroughbred handicapping.

"Everybody's by somebody and out of somebody. See, that's the thing about you and me. We don't know who we're by and out of. If you were by Round Table or Stage Door Johnny, for instance, that would mean you could run well on grass."

Toni had heard that we were adoptive brothers and was intrigued. I had previously found that it made me more interesting to some women to reveal this part of my background.

"I can't believe you haven't tried to find your birth parents," she said.

"The records are sealed," I said.

"But don't you ever wonder who you are?"

"We know who we are," said Sterling.

Toni shook her head.

"I'd be on 'Unsolved Mysteries' so fast," she said.

"We have a mother," said Sterling. "And I wish you could get her out here once to visit," he added to me. "She'd like it. Those are hibachis down there by the pool, y'know."

"Uh-huh."

"I've got a good career, y'know."

"His clients do better on their interviews than any of our other counselors' do," said Toni.

"I sent her that article in the Register about my promotion, with my picture," he said. "But it's like she's been lamenting over me for fifteen years."

"She does that with me too," I admitted.

"She's living in the past. I don't live in the past. I live in the now." He lowered his voice. "Actually, that's all they've got out here, is the now."

"Well, good. I used to worry about you, after—you know."

He snorted and spoke to Toni. "He means 'Manhattan Live.' He won't say it." Then, back to me: "That's a whole life ago. Do I look like I fell apart over that?"

I shook my head, and he went on more quietly.

"I'm not saying it didn't bother me. For a while there right afterward I used to replay it. I couldn't figure it out. Why did I say 'Manson'?"

Another girl gingerly got into the water below us, and the guy in the pool skidded water at her with his hand, splashing her. She squealed and laughed.

"I remember back then, I asked Lee Ann—you know, she took some courses," said Sterling. "Asked her why she thought I did it. First she said it was a parapraxis—Freudian slip. I subconsciously didn't want to be an actor, so I made myself fail."

I was doubtful. "But why would your subconscious want to hurt your conscious so much?"

"That's what *I* said. I told her she was full of shit and she said that was a very revealing remark, you know how that analytical talk goes. Then another time she told me that with the blindfold on, knowing my birth mother and father might be watching, I returned to the womb and went through the process of being born again, and that destroyed my power of speech."

"Wow," I said, impressed. "But then why didn't you just say 'ga'?"

"That's what *I* said! Babies can't say 'Manson.' Then later she said Freud was a discredited doctrinaire quack. So we went back to the Art Klee theory.... Now she's into religion."

He and I drank our Diet Pepsis. Toni had white wine. The guy down in the pool was still splashing water in the face of the new girl, who was laughing but telling him to stop.

"Klee had no right to talk like that to you," I said. "You want my opinion, you were better than he is. You were more creative."

Sterling laughed, a short one.

"Saying the wrong line is not creative."

"You made one mistake and then you stopped. You shouldn't have listened to him."

Sterling showed annoyance for the first time.

"If a soldier," he said quietly, "while running away from the enemy, trips and falls and shoots two of his own guys ... how many times do you think he should get to do that?"

Down in the pool the girl said, "Hey, really, cut it out, Craig."

"You were distracted," I said.

"A real actor," said Sterling, "can say his lines while they're throwing produce."

He rose and pitched his Pepsi can into a sack

he had hanging from the knob on the balcony door.

"I make more money now than I ever would've made otherwise. I help people. The world needs me more than it ever needed another actor."

"Right," said Toni.

"I just think, you know, you used to like to do that," I said. "He was really good," I told Toni. "He could've been in these Art Klee movies, only they'd have been Sterling Fleger movies."

Sterling looked down at the kid in the pool, who was still splashing the girl. "Why don't you cut it out?" he called down.

The kid looked up and said, "Whyn't you kiss my ass?"

"Oh, jeez," said Toni.

Sterling looked like a lightbulb had gone on over his head. He strode back into the living room, turned, faced the window and the balcony and us, and ran out, right between Toni and me. He leapt up onto the balcony railing and poised for a second, wobbling on the black iron. I grabbed at him but he jumped, out over the concrete courtyard, into the night.

The two girls in the pool screamed. Toni and I stood leaning over the railing, left behind, watching him go out and down.

He made it into the pool, landing between the diving board and one corner, in a cannonball. There was an explosive geyser of water, then silence as he bobbed back up to the surface.

"The fuck's the *matter* with you?" yelled the kid, treading water a few feet away from him.

A man stormed out of the ground-floor office below us.

"I saw that, that's it," he said. He was tall and lanky, with hair that was clearly thinning from where we sat. "You're outta here, Fleger."

Sterling bobbed in the deep end, wiping his eyes and nose with one hand, looking up.

"Why?" he asked.

The lanky man pointed to a sign on the barred pool gate.

"No diving off the balconies. I told you, you want to kill yourself, do it somewhere else."

"If I wanted to kill myself, I would've landed on the concrete," Sterling said. "This guy wanted me to kiss his ass so I hustled on down here."

"Are you fuckin' *nuts*?" asked the kid in the pool.

"You mean you didn't mean it?" asked Sterling. "You mean it was like, an insult?"

There was a pause, while the kid and Sterling treaded water in the deep end, thirty-seven-year-old Sterling in his shirt and shorts. The kid thought it over and then swam to the shallow end and hauled himself out of the water, muttering unintelligibly. He walked away, shouting "Asshole!" over his shoulder once.

"That's a very revealing remark!" Sterling called after him. Then he crawled up out of the deep end and began talking to the lanky man. Toni, standing beside me, shook her head.

"Was he like this when you were kids?" she asked.

"You mean he's like this now?"

"He's really sweet, but he's way unhappy. I don't see him as long-term for that reason."

I looked down at my brother, explaining himself to the landlord, the water dripping from his clothes. He had missed the concrete by about a foot.

CHAPTER FIVE

In 1989, a baseball pitcher named Donnie Moore killed himself in Anaheim. People said he had never recovered from getting booed incessantly by California Angels fans for throwing a home-run pitch in the 1986 playoffs.

His death inspired a woman named Katie Curtis to start a support group for people who had had a public disaster. It's called Public Setback Support. The members of the group call it Piss, or Fuck-ups Anonymous.

Those names are unfair to the memory of Donnie Moore, whose home-run pitch, if you ever saw it on TV, wasn't even that bad. But there are plenty of folks with more cause for embarrassment, and some of them have joined up with Katie Curtis.

In 1990 there was only one PSS chapter, and it held its meetings in Laguna Beach, a coastal town next to Irvine. People came from all over to attend. By the time I arrived in California, there were members from as far north as San Francisco. There was a piece about the group in the paper a week after my arrival. I took it to the Dittmer's Employment offices in Irvine to show Sterling.

He sat at his desk while I held up my index finger and read a quote from Katie Curtis: "We meet to let ourselves know that a setback is not a death."

I handed him the article.

"Support groups work," I said. "I'm proof."

He tilted back in his black leather chair and gazed at me. He wore a tie and suspenders. The chair was too small for him. He nodded, thoughtfully.

"So I'm a failure," he said.

"No, but I saw you jump in the pool and I think you're a little fucked up."

"If I was fucked up, I wouldn't've made it."

"If you weren't fucked up, you wouldn't've tried it."

Sterling sniffed once, something he does when he's tiring of a subject.

"I'm fine, A.J." He gestured to indicate his office. "Don't improve me."

"That landlord wants you out, doesn't he?"

Sterling said nothing.

"You're afraid to watch Nick at Nite."

His eyes flashed.

"That's a lie!"

"You can't watch anything from when we were kids."

"Why would I want to? That stuff was no good."

"You can't watch 'Manhattan Live' or 'Saturday Night Live' either. Or Letterman, because he might have Art Klee on. Every channel—ouch, ouch, ouch."

Sterling smiled appreciatively.

"That's good," he said. "Nice to hear from you, up there on your promontory of success. This summer, if *your* dream comes true, we'll be able to hear you at Wrigley Field, going, 'Getcha program.' "

"Yeah," I shot back, "and I'm gonna do just like you. If I say it wrong once, I'll quit."

Sterling got up, so I made a dignified exit. Little brothers learn when to say things. We were in his place of business. I didn't run. If I'd heard him behind me, I would've.

Turns out that after I left, he read the article because he saw Eddie Friend's name in it. Eddie Friend was one of Sterling's old Top Ten Favorite Actors. He was in a secret agent series during our key viewing years, and had a nice carefree style which Sterling used to emulate when he got in and out of the family car. In the late eighties, though, Friend took to getting high in public. He made a fool of himself twice on "The Tonight Show," and he got into a shouting match from the stage with an audience member during a disease telethon. In the tabloid photos afterward he always looked drunk, although he might just have been blinking. His airtime was curtailed. Later he got over his substance abuse, but he'd never quite recovered from his embarrassment. He was a founding member of Public Setback Support.

Sterling loved Eddie Friend. To Sterling, the man had nothing to apologize for. He didn't mind pretending to be a failure if he could meet Eddie Friend.

Laguna Beach is a beautiful little town with ocean on one side and hills on the other, down which the finer homes sometimes slide during rainy winters. It has a lot of art galleries and other little shops. Bette Davis used to go there to relax after a tough shoot. I believe Bette Midler and the guy who plays Freddie Krueger have houses there now.

Laguna Canyon Road is snaky; it narrows and widens from two lanes to three and back to two as it slithers inland. The little building that housed PSS was set back from one of the curviest parts of the road, and on the night we went, we drove past it once and had to catch it on the return.

Sterling groused most of the way, about the road, the driving, the waste of time. He muttered on across the parking lot and into the building, a pillbox with a sign in front that said Public Setback Support. Inside was a VFW hall-type room with long tables and folding chairs.

We came in unobtrusively and sat down. Then we gawked for a while. Several of the members looked familiar.

I recognized Katie Curtis from the paper. I also spotted Wrong-Way Ohanian, the Denver place-kicker who picked up a fumbled snap in a playoff game and ran sixty-five yards to score for Buffalo.

There was Frank Chenelle, the golfer who seized up on the green in the U.S. Open and addressed his ball like the Tin Man of Oz. Mason Murray, an ex-congressman, made a lightbulb joke on "20/20" that demeaned over two-thirds of the world's population. There were about thirty people altogether, all of whom, as Ohanian said, had fucked up in public. Many had met their downfall on a smaller stage, with an audience of hundreds or thousands rather than millions. But they had all done something that followed them around.

"This is the first support group to focus exclusively on public humiliation," said Katie Curtis, a good-looking fiftyish blond woman at the far end of the room. "People think embarrassment is trivial, but even normies have nightmares about it. They dream about being out on the street naked, or disgracing themselves at work. The difference with us is, we've lived the dream.

"First principle: You had to be good to begin with or you wouldn't be here. Most people don't get the chance to screw up as openly as we did."

Sterling spotted Eddie Friend right away, of course, sitting across the room. It thrilled me to see him too—a real star. He looked heavier than I remembered, but terrific, with that polished, mahogany leading-man skin. He had his own hair too.

Katie Curtis asked if there were any newcomers and told us to stand up and say our first names and where we were from. There were two or three, including Sterling. The one who stood up next to Mason Murray held my attention for the rest of the night.

It wasn't that Abby Zane was spectacularly beautiful. She was just beautiful. She was small, with short black hair and a dark, sad face and what I believe are called almond eyes. She had a big smile which lit up and transfigured her face, although I didn't find that out right away. She was searching for this smile while she tried to make light of her story.

She was a singer. She'd become lost in the Canadien national anthem prior to a hockey game in Winnipeg, and in trying to extricate herself from the lyric tangle, she'd tossed in a few words from one or another of *our* patriotic songs, which the crowd had found condescending. The whole incident as she described it made me wish I knew her well enough to sit beside her until she got over it.

"I apologized in the paper," she said. "But I still got this hate mail."

I seethed in my seat, hearing this.

"Have they thrown shit on your lawn?" asked Wrong-Way Ohanian. "Because until they have, you don't deserve to be here."

"Wrong-w— Larry," warned Katie Curtis.

"It's not the abuse that bothers me so much as the fear," said Abby Zane. "I'm afraid of screwing up again."

"At least you *can* screw up again," said Ohanian. "You can sing anywhere. What am *I* gonna do—kick field goals in some small bistro?"

"I think," said Eddie Friend, speaking for the first time, "the sooner the better."

"What?" said Abby.

"Sing," said Friend. "Doesn't have to be much. But the longer you wait, the tougher it gets."

There was applause from the others. This was apparently customary—encouragement to get back on the horse right there at the meeting. I glanced at Sterling; he was attentive. I winced in advance. Ever since "Manhattan Live" I've been squeamish about live acts.

Abby did some deep breathing. She took some color into her face. Then she grimaced and shook her head.

"I really don't want to do this," she said.

They all waited. She looked at Katie Curtis, looked at the floor, and finally raised her head.

"This is by Gershwin," she said.

She began tentatively, and her voice quavered a couple of times. If you don't recall the tune, it's a pretty melody, a parody love song of the twenties or thirties. At the tempo she took, it was poignant. The lyric is satirical of other love song lyrics and goes like this:

Blah blah blah blah moon
Blah blah blah above
Blah blah blah blah croon
Blah blah blah blah love

Tra-la-la-la
Tra-la lalala
Merry month of May
Tra-la-la-la
Tra-la lalala
'Neath the skies of gray

Blah blah blah your hair
Blah blah blah your eyes
Blah blah blah blah care
Blah blah blah blah skies

Tra-la la-la
Tra-la lalala cottage for two

Blah blah blah blah blah
Darling with you

During the first verse, Sterling whispered, "She's *not* very good on words, is she?"

"Those *are* the words, you simp," I hissed back.

"Oh. Well, not bad, then."

I've always liked Gershwin. Mom used to play "American in Paris" and "Rhapsody in Blue" on the record player to put me to sleep when I was little, and I learned some George and Ira tunes when I had my piano lessons. "Blah Blah Blah" is a minor standard. But I'd never known it to be powerful and touching until that night.

She got more confident as she went along and turned her quaver into a little bit of vibrato. She didn't have the richest voice of all time, but she put heart into those blahs. She made my chest hurt. I think I might've said "Ow."

She was quietly pleased with the applause afterward; excited, I think. "You'll notice the lyric's pretty easy on that one," she said.

"Step at a time," nodded Katie Curtis.

She asked if any newcomers wanted to share. One guy said his name was Max and he'd balled up a major speech at a convention. I don't remember the details of his downfall because I was dividing my attention between Abby Zane and Sterling, wondering whether he was going to speak. "We're here to share our experience, strength and hope," Katie Curtis had said—a direct steal from AA.

Sterling was shifting restlessly. I didn't know if he thought it was all crap or not. He hummed tonelessly a couple of times during Max's testimony. When Max finished, Katie Curtis asked if any other newcomer wanted to share.

There was a longish silence, but no one seemed to find it uncomfortable. People waited.

"My name is Sterling," said Sterling, "and I'm a fuckup."

"Hi, Sterling," said everyone.

He told the "Manhattan Live" story briefly. When he was done, Wrong-Way Ohanian was unimpressed.

"I don't think this guy qualifies," he said. "One blown line fifteen years ago. Nobody knew him then and nobody knows him now. Bruise pretty easy, don't ya, Jack?"

"Wait a minute," said Katie Curtis. "I remember that bit. I saw it not long ago on Channel 12, on reruns. I *wondered* what was going on in that. Now I get it: You were supposed to say Charles *Boyer*." She seemed delighted at clearing up this old mystery. "Well, that would've worked, wouldn't it?"

"Yeah," Sterling allowed, with a little laugh. "Yeah, that would've worked."

"How about that?" said Katie Curtis. "So what are you up to now, Sterling?"

"Well, I'm doing okay, I coach job interview-ees."

"How do you like it?"

"Fine. Fine." He paused for a moment, and then looked at Abby Zane. "You shamed me just now," he said. "I never tried again. They told me to get out and I got out. So ever since, I've had two things I'm not proud of. It's funny, when I started I was gonna be everybody. Now I just wish I'd fought my way back there and said one line right. You hate to go out on 'Manson.' "

"He could be anybody," I broke in. "He could even do a building with all the things going on on the different floors."

"This is my brother," said Sterling. "He has no life of his own."

"So all you want is one more chance," said Wrong-Way Ohanian. "Well, forget it."

"What Larry means," said Katie Curtis, "is that most of us will never perform for our old audience again. We're here to deal with that and move on, whether in the same field or a new one."

"If you don't mind my asking," said Sterling, "what happened to you? You look familiar but I don't . . ."

"I was anchoring the news when an earthquake hit," she said, "and I lost my poise. I'm sure you've seen me on the blooper shows."

She mimed her famous scream. You've probably seen it. They showed it all over the country.

"Well, that could've happened to anybody," said Sterling.

"That's our motto," acknowledged Katie

Curtis. "You're welcome to do a little something, if you care to."

"Doesn't have to be a big soliloquy," said Eddie Friend to Sterling. "Something simple. An improv."

Sterling shook his head. "I don't think—"

"Do 'Kicking the Habit,' " I said, and turned to Friend. "He does a guy who's trying not to—"

"Shut up, you'll kill it," said Sterling peremptorily. "You're just like Mom."

"Well, do it."

"I haven't done it in fifteen years."

"It's a *mime*. How can you go wrong?"

Sterling gazed at me. I knew what he was thinking, but once again it was a situation where he couldn't really slug me. The rest of the group waited. You got the feeling they'd survive whether he did it or not. Sterling took in a deep breath, as Abby Zane had.

"It's a guy alone, cold turkey in his apartment," he said finally.

He walked to the end of the room, where there was a space with some chairs and a long table. He cleared his throat, made as if to start, stopped and cleared his throat again, although it was unnecessary since he wasn't going to speak. It occurred to me that maybe it was just as well he was now in another line of work.

Then he started, hesitantly at first. He gradually became this young guy. He came in a door, stuffed his hands in his pockets and walked around. He made you see his kitchen and living room as he paced back and forth, looking distractedly in cabinets and refrigerator, turning on the TV, sitting down, getting up, turning it off, becoming increasingly agitated and miserable as the single thing on his mind became imperative.

He kept his hands in his pockets when walking—in fact, he forced them down except when using them to open a can of beer or trying to concentrate on a magazine. Then he tried concentrating on a *dirty* magazine, but that didn't help either. He did some calisthenics, but seemed to lose control over his arms and had to stop. He made himself sit at the kitchen table and be still. His eyes closed. He broke into a sweat.

His right hand emerged from its pocket but he put it back. It came out again, and he used his left hand to jam it down. It came out again, and the hands began to battle—the right trying to come up, the left pushing the right back down. His face became distorted as he fought himself.

Gradually, he began to lose. The right hand pushed up, up, up, against the left—against the man himself. And finally, suddenly, the right hand won, and he picked his nose with such violence that he threw himself off the chair.

I just can't resist that bit. I guess I was just the right age when he first did it. This time around, I was impressed with how precise his hand movements were despite the long layoff. As he came back to his chair to laughter and polite applause, he cast a quick look at Eddie Friend. When he saw Friend smiling, Sterling took a deep breath and his eyes welled up. I think it was one of those breakthroughs.

Mason Murray was unimpressed.

"Don't they do talkies now?" he asked.

"He can do a lot more than that," I said indignantly. "He can do drama or whatever, comedy or anything."

"Well, if you're thinking we could use our influence for him," said a guy who hadn't spoken before, "you haven't got the idea of the group. We don't have any influence. That's one of the reasons we're here."

"He doesn't belong here," said Wrong-Way Ohanian flatly. "Nobody knows what he did. This group is for people who got shit thrown on their lawn."

"Again with the shit on the lawn," murmured Murray.

Ohanian addressed Sterling directly.

"You don't qualify because nobody *knows* what a fuckup you are," he said. "They came after me and ran me out of town. They would've killed me if they could've."

"So he's not in your league," I said. "He's still a fuckup."

"Yeah," said Sterling stoutly. "I got a right to be here."

"You're welcome anytime, Sterling," said Katie Curtis.

In the parking lot afterward, Sterling spoke briefly to Eddie Friend and I saw that I had to approach Abby Zane immediately. I'd been accepted at one meeting as a guest, but I had no excuse to attend any more. I was just a regular fuckup, not a standout. If she got away now, I'd never see her again.

I caught up to her at her car. It was chilly, and I could see her breath as she turned to face me. I won't say it looked better than anyone else's, but it made her seem, I don't know, warm and vulnerable, the way it came out and disappeared. She was bright-eyed from her success.

I said, "I liked your singing."

"Thank you," she said. "I liked your brother's routine."

"Well, he's very good," I said absently. I'd lost interest in him.

"I liked the way you pitched him, too," she said. "Showed a good heart."

It was my turn to clear my throat. It seemed everyone had to muscle up and perform tonight.

"I was hoping we could get together for lunch or something," I said. "Maybe discuss song selection."

"Well," she said, "I have a rule. I don't go out with anyone unless I'm sure they're not crazy. I had a bad experience, so . . ."

I searched my mind frantically for references.

"The people who know I'm okay are in Illinois . . . Sterling," I called, "come over here and tell someone I'm not crazy."

"He's not," said Sterling, coming up beside me. "We have an affidavit."

"Don't do that," I muttered.

"Well, maybe I'll see you at the next meeting." She smiled at us and got in her car, and Sterling knocked me ten feet sideways.

"*God*, I feel great," he said as I regained my balance. "You were right to bring me here. I think I've had an epiphany. I know what I want again."

"Well, gee, that's swell, Ster, but who *cares*, you know? I mean, I know what *I* want in life now too, only I don't have her number and there she goes and I don't know where she lives."

"Sure you do," said Sterling, and pointed at her license plate, which said "Lugunuh."

That meeting led to everything good and bad for Sterling and me. I'd have to say it was the most pivotal event of my life since you and I parted company, and it put Sterling on the road to his showdown on the Strip. Abby drove home humming "Blah Blah Blah."

CHAPTER SIX

After doing his mime at the PSS meeting, Sterling found himself facing one of those thorny life choices—dream vs. paycheck. He could dive back into acting at thirty-five in hopes of someday saying one line right on national TV, or he could continue making a living. To help him decide, he chose to advise me on how to win over Abby Zane. He took my desire for her as a kind of parallel, an omen for himself—he figured that if I could succeed with an intelligent, attractive woman, there might be a miracle in store for him too. The next morning, before I even called her, he took me to the video room at Dittmer's, the room in which he taped and coached his clients.

"Let's say she agrees to lunch," he said. "You have to impress her at that first meeting, and your problem is you've got no drive. Your attitude has always been, they should build a zoo around you and toss in the meat. Women hate that. You have to radiate energy. Stand over there and give me Vitality."

I put one leg up on a chair and leaned over it, smiling into the camera like Howard Keel, the hearty woodsman.

He looked at the monitor and rubbed his face.

"Okay. We'll make your disadvantages assets. You've got a weaselly quality; we'll make you intense." He spoke to me softly, in a kind of throb. "Keep your voice low. You have to bring her head forward. Get her to *focus* on you, pull her in . . ."

"No," I said. "I think she's had bad luck with intense."

"Oh. Okay. Good. Thank God for the guy previous, huh? Just gimme Sincere then."

"How?"

He made the lines on his forehead crosshatch and pointed at them.

"I can't get that design," I said.

He erased Sincere and gave me Irked.

"You don't bring much to the party, do you?"

"Those are just tricks," I said. "You used to go a lot deeper."

"Hey, Beaver: From a standing start, which of us would do better with this girl—me with the tricks, or you without them?"

"We'll never know, will we?" I said evenly.

There was a pause.

"I can't work with you," he said finally, "if you won't take direction."

"Okay. I'll just have to do it my way."

"You don't *have* a way," he pointed out. "You need a plan here, A.J. Improv is sloppy. Nine out of ten improvs stink. You must prepare. This is *mating*. If you haven't got an act, she won't give you a job stacking chairs. That's what I tell my clients and that's what I'm telling you."

"I think she wants someone who *is* what he *says* he is."

Sterling exhaled.

"Fine. 'Be yourself.' Sitcom advice."

Abby was politely cordial on the phone. She couldn't do lunch, but offered an invitation to her upcoming singing engagement at a ski lodge in the mountains near Lake Arrowhead.

"I'm working Friday and Saturday night," she said. "Do you ski?"

"Sure."

"Well, it's open to the public."

"Great. What are you going to sing?"

"Oh, mostly standards. I just work in the small lounge, with the house band. No anthems."

I laughed agreeably, thinking, Sterling was right. I can't even talk.

"I hope I didn't sound like 'Send your résumé' in the parking lot," she said.

"No, not at all."

"It's just that you have to be careful."

"Oh, hey," I agreed.

"There's so much to check off with a guy anymore. Is he controlling, is he a leech? Is he a ticking bomb?"

"Well, one thing I'm not is a ticking bomb," I

assured her. "I know what it does to a family."

"Oh, really?"

"Yeah, my dad was like that."

"Was he?"

"Oh, yeah. You never knew when he was going to go off."

There was silence on the other end.

"Of course, he wasn't my real dad," I added quickly.

Sterling was right about the dangers of not rehearsing. By the time Abby hung up, she was pretty sure I was Ticking Bomb Junior and I was pretty sure it was a waste of time to go to the ski lodge. I went anyhow, but as I drove Sterling's car up there, I felt the way I used to when I approached the home of someone who wasn't going to want my encyclopedias.

There is nothing funny about skiing. I've seen it treated comically, and if you watch it from a distance you can enjoy the falls. But people get badly injured, even die. I think it's a disservice to the novice to make it seem amusing.

On TV, when you see the experts ski, they don't seem to be doing much—just swinging their hips. They've got poles to steer with. They just lean this way and that, kind of skate down the hill.

The way I saw it, I hadn't really lied to Abby about being able to ski. I figured I could. I could run down a hill, so I thought I ought to be able to slide down one.

I drove Sterling's car up into the mountains and got to the lodge early on Friday afternoon. There

was a sign on an easel in the lobby, with the name of the band and Abby's picture.

She was there already, near the ski shop, with a tall guy she introduced as Ken Bender, a reporter for channel something or other. I wouldn't say she was warm to me, but I was glad she even shook hands after that phone conversation.

"I'm only going down the intermediate slope today," she said. "All I need is to wipe out. I can't sing on painkillers, or I *can,* but I'm the only one who likes it."

Ken Bender and I laughed.

"Maybe we'll see you out there," she said.

They left and I snuck around here and there, renting equipment and asking how to put it on.

Once I got up on the skis outside, I coasted carefully on the flat for a few minutes and then glided over to the intermediate hill. They had a tow-rope; you grabbed it and it pulled you. I wasn't prepared for the speed going up the incline. That should have told me something.

The intermediate was a straightforward slope with a couple of bumps in it. People were descending without incident, people just like me—men, women, teenage kids. They were gliding down, side to side, in about, oh, thirty seconds, and then at the bottom they would either coast on to the lodge or veer off to the left to take the towrope back up. The only people falling were the ones moving from the towrope to the starting place atop the hill. It was pretty slippery up there, and awkward.

I didn't fall, though. I got from the towrope to the starting place without incident by deftly using

my ski poles. That gave me some confidence.

From the summit, the slope looked steeper than it had from the bottom. The thought flickered into my head that I might not be ready. But there were people behind me, so I took a deep breath and went straight down the hill.

When I say straight down I am not just talking big. I had neglected to learn that side-to-side movement which allows skiers to decelerate, and consequently I shot down the slope like a hawk coming down on a field mouse.

Another skier, a woman, was weaving along sedately below me. She was like a child picking daisies on the train track. I ran her down.

We landed in a tangle, halfway down the hill. I'm afraid it hurt her more than it did me; she hadn't known I was coming and I had, so I was more braced. I tried to help her up but she slapped at me and my apologies, so I quit. She righted herself and continued to the bottom, and I staggered over toward the towrope.

It only went up. I considered squatting and sliding down the hill from where I was, but just then I saw Abby Zane gracefully descending the slope past me, with Ken Bender behind her. He didn't knock her down.

I thought of Sterling, quitting after one failure and staying on the bench for fifteen years. I grabbed the towrope and it yanked me back up to the top.

That side-to-side thing *seemed* simple enough. Something involving the knees and leaning, maybe with a little jump in there somewhere. I had snow down the back of my neck and inside my socks, but

I was throbbing with adrenaline, mortification and proximity to Abby. So when I started down the hill this time, I actually went faster than before.

I still couldn't get that weaving thing. It just didn't come. I kept my balance all right, but I couldn't brake; I just accelerated. The only thing likely to slow me down was the equipment rental shed at the bottom.

This occurred to me in the two or three seconds it took to shoot halfway down the hill, where I hit another bump and picked up speed.

I guess I panicked. I had seen other skiers use their ski poles to slow their momentum, so I stabbed my pole into the snow in front of me. Unfortunately I put it down between my skis.

Hitting that pole was one of the electrifying moments of my life. I recoiled from the groin and started turning somersaults and cartwheels. I bounced and caromed down the hill, head over heels over skis. I don't remember if I screamed or not.

I finally came to a stop in a twisted heap at the bottom. My final posture was on my back, with my legs pointing back up the hill, at the feet of Abby Zane and Ken Bender. I saw Abby's face, upside down, peering down at me.

"Are you all *right?*" she asked in an awed, low voice.

I didn't hurt at all, which saddened me. If I didn't hurt after a fall like that, the likelihood was that I had broken my neck.

"I wish we could have known each other better," I said.

She crouched beside me and someone lifted me under the arms. As she helped me to my feet, I had an odd, reminiscent feeling. A dizziness and a euphoria, a feeling of arrival.

I thought, I'm Rob Petrie. This is just like the opening of "The Dick Van Dyke Show."

Ken Bender was an expressionless guy with a reddish face and a heavy mustache. He talked like a character in a hard-hitting film. He and Abby helped me into the lounge, and the way I looked got him talking about corpses he'd seen in his days as a police reporter and relatives he'd had to interview after tragedies. I got the impression Abby had heard most of it already. "Ken's seen a lot of life," she said. "He's going to be an anchorman in New Orleans."

I tried various movements on the couch when we sat down, and determined that I was miraculously unhurt.

Abby laughed merrily at the recollection of my descent. "Since you weren't killed, I have to tell you, you were really funny."

"Wish I'd seen it," I said with dignity.

"You looked like a rolling swastika," said Ken Bender. That still ranks as one of the oddest remarks I've ever heard in a conversation.

"It's hard to believe you didn't break anything," said Abby.

"Isn't it?" I said. "I guess I must have been spared for some great purpose."

That night I sat with Bender as Abby sang with the band. The musicians were jazzmen and split their repertoire between new-age instrumentals and old standards. On the oldies, Abby would sing two verses and then they'd elaborate for three minutes and she'd sing the last verse.

"So you're what?" Bender asked me. "After her?"

"I like her," I admitted.

"She deserves the best," he said.

"That may be, but I'm gonna try anyway."

"We were together briefly," he volunteered after a few moments, "but she needs someone who can put her first. My work has to come first, otherwise I can't do it the way it has to be done."

"I know what you mean," I said. "I'm an ice cream taster."

We didn't talk after that, and I was able to concentrate on Abby. She was singing with confidence and her phrasing was fine, but whenever she started a song with tricky or hard-to-remember words, I squirmed in my seat. There weren't more than twenty people in the small lounge, but I didn't want her to have a semi-public setback so soon after her big one in Canada.

I thought she might be in trouble at the beginning of the band's version of "They Can't Take That Away from Me." You probably remember the song—it starts out "The way you wear your hat/ The way you sip your tea." It's tricky because you have to remember several different "the way you's." She seemed unsure of the first verse, so I decided to act out the lines there at our table, to kind of guide her. It was Gershwin again, so I knew it.

At the appropriate time I held up my knife for

"The way you hold your knife," and I caught her eye and she sang that line okay. But I turned out to be more of a distraction than a help. On "The way your smile just beams," I pointed at my smile, but she sang, "The way your teeth just . . . what are you doing?" which was way off. After that she didn't look at me.

I felt bad for messing her up. But here's the strange thing. At the end of the set she came to the table and sat between Bender and me, and she smiled at me and said, "Hey, Harpo."

I've since learned that women find certain kinds of male ineptitude endearing—although there are areas where they won't tolerate it.

She had an experimental dinner with me back in Laguna a few days later. Two nights after that we had dinner again. Then it became time for me to burn brighter or fade away, back to Illinois.

"There's no relationship if the sex isn't good," she remarked during the second dinner.

"It's better, I think, to get right to it," I said, nodding. "Otherwise, you can build it up until it's almost sure to be a letdown."

"Maybe you're right," she said. "Maybe we should do it now, while we don't have any expectations."

She had, after all, seen me stick the ski pole between my legs.

Abby lived in a tiny one-room cottage in Laguna Canyon, with a potbellied stove in the middle of the room. The bathroom and shower were outside; she shared them with two neighbors. Housing in Laguna Beach was very expensive and this was the only way for her to afford it on her singer/word processor earnings. The place was no bigger than a garage, but it was warm and comfortable. We went back there after the second dinner and faced the moment.

Abby was a little edgy. She had had two glasses of wine. She was steeling herself.

"I like you a lot," she said, "or I wouldn't do this. You have a sweet quality. But if it doesn't work out, we just let it go. No bad feelings, nobody's fault. You can't be shadowing me or anything."

"All right," I said. "But you have to agree to leave me alone if it turns out that *you're* really bad."

There was no room in her room for a bed. She unfolded a futon couch onto the floor. We stood looking down at it.

"Not very fancy," she said.

I didn't agree. To me, it was the terminus of my ambition.

I was nervous, though. It occurred to me that the possibilities of male sexual performance correspond to what football coach Woody Hayes once said about the forward pass: Only three things can happen and two of them are bad. You can either be underexcited, overexcited, or just right.

Fortunately, Abby obliterated the underexcited possibility by taking off her clothes and reclining on the futon. In the flickering light from the stove, she was sculpture, curvaceous and stunning. Some women look better in clothes, and I'm not saying Abby didn't look good dressed. It's just that she looked great on the futon.

I got my own clothes off all right and was just coming in for a landing when Abby stopped me by asking, "Do you have anything?"

I looked down at her, a little wounded.

"Are you blind?"

"No, I mean do you have any diseases or anything."

"No," I said. "And if you don't mind my saying, I think you should've asked earlier."

The lucky thing was that her introduction of the viral or venereal theme put just enough of a lid on my passion that I was able to avoid the over-excited possibility, and we hit it off. She let herself go completely; it was as if she suddenly trusted me. We made a good team. We were an opening night success. I was so amazed to be where I was that I was ready on call the rest of the night. Abby seemed pleased about that until about two o'clock.

The next morning she told me that it had gone better than she expected, and it occurred to me that men with unspectacular exteriors have one great advantage over the heroic-looking types. A hunk can either perform up to his looks or disappoint; he can't exceed his outward appearance. But on a good night, the rest of us can surprise.

Sterling helped me find a job photographing houses for a real estate magazine, and I resolved to go upward from there. I called Mom and told her I was staying in California for a while to pursue a career.

"You'd better hurry," she said.

In March, Abby declared she would never

marry unless she felt free to follow whatever calling she chose, and that anyone who expected her to cook for him was deluded. I said she could marry me as much or as little as she wanted.

"Well," she admitted, "you're checked off on the other points."

She talked to Mom on the phone, and the conversation seemed to go all right. Later I asked Mom what she'd told Abby about me.

"I said you had a good heart and up to now you hadn't amounted to much, but of my two sons you were the one I'd recommend as a husband and father."

"Well, I'll have to get a bigger hat, won't I?"

"I couldn't very well say you were a pathologist at Billings Hospital. She seemed satisfied. She seemed very nice."

I met Abby's parents and grandfather, who lived in Anaheim Hills. They were Republicans, but I liked the grandfather, a distinguished-looking old guy who worked in waste water treatment. He had been shot down over Germany in WW2. Before he was captured, he walked through the Black Forest in a daze, singing, "When will I ever find/The girl who is on my mind/The girl who is my ideal?"

Her father and mother didn't seem delighted with my prospects, but I was used to that reaction. Their attitude seemed to be that Abby had always been the headstrong daughter with the shack in the canyon, and so I was about what might be expected.

We were married in July, in a public gazebo overlooking the ocean in Laguna. It was very windy that day, but sunny too. Mom came out from Henley. Sterling was my best man.

The Zanes threw a small reception at the Las Brisas restaurant. Sterling was there with Toni Boyce, although they weren't getting along. Toni confided that he'd been getting testier at work. Sterling seemed happy at the party, though. He took me aside and told me I was lucky. Abby was exuberant, chatty, delighted to see her pals and relatives.

We honeymooned in San Francisco and Sausalito and came back to rent a small house up the canyon in Laguna. Maggie was born June 19, 1991. I've got her picture right here in front of me, and several more on the bookcase. I'll enclose some.

On that day as a kid when I looked out the window and told Grandma Jessie, "I want something but I don't know what I want," I think I had a longing for something to give my heart to. Because when I found Abby and when Maggie was born, I felt that old childhood ache come back and burst inside me. My own family filled me up. I found the sense of my life in them.

Of course, then I had worries.

CHAPTER SEVEN

After I married Abby and moved the last of my stuff out of Sterling's apartment, he went to his boss at Dittmer's and asked for a leave of absence. The boss replied that if by "leave of absence" Sterling meant leaving his job with no likelihood of ever getting it back, why, sure, he could have a leave of absence.

Sterling hurled himself back into acting as hard as he'd hurled himself into his apartment complex swimming pool. And after four years—by the summer of 1994—he had accomplished the following:

• He'd been in several plays in a storefront theater in Fullerton called the Actors' Bunker, some of which had been favorably reviewed but none of which had been attended by more than twenty-five people at a time. He was excellent in a Japanese play about a small-town barber, and he never froze or said the wrong line in a performance, but he didn't crow; he said his heart could differentiate between an audience of twenty-five and one of 25 million, and it beat accordingly.

• He had appeared in a West Coast TV commercial for slacks, shot in the contemporary jerky fashion which suggests the cameraman is being savagely beaten while filming. All that showed of Sterling in the finished spot was one ear, one eye, one pants leg and his butt.

• He had a screaming victim role in a special effects horror movie, getting turned inside out by a tentacled alien. "The only direction I got," he told me, "was 'Have fun with it' and 'Keep your mouth open.'"

• He went to stuntman school, joined the Stuntmen's Association and did some doubling to augment his income. He learned about ratchets—the line-and-harness contraption that jerks you backward when you're shot—and the air-ram, which sends you flying after you've been blown up. He was killed several times in lower-budget films in 1993 and early '94.

"Keeps you going while you're waiting for that breakthrough part," he said philosophically. He would acknowledge that things were going slowly. "I don't have a lot to point to yet . . . I can't say, 'Well, did you catch me in *Slugs,* when the creature tore my stomach out through my mouth?'" He believed that actors weren't as important to filmmakers as they used to be: "They can VR you, or morph you, or animate the whole thing. A human being's pretty tame. But it's all right. I never did pay my dues the first time around." He liked the camaraderie with the other performers at the Actors' Bunker. He said it was like being on a team.

While Sterling strove and scuffled around the periphery of Hollywood, I was the one who got discovered. My career finally found me.

From the day of Maggie's birth, I carried on like the world's first father. I bought a video camera and shot long sequences of her rolling from one side of the living room to the other. I wrote her letters of parental wisdom that she could read when I died. And I worried. No one had prepared me for the worrying. I didn't remember my parents worrying, although they must have.

It was a whole new form of anxiety for me, unprecedented. I loved Abby as much as Maggie, but Abby was grown up and strong. I only really feared for her when she was out somewhere and late getting home. Maggie was tiny and fragile, an ectomorph, and pale like me. Whenever she got sick and didn't eat for a day she became transparent.

As I told you, she got the croup. The books say croup isn't usually as bad as it sounds, and that's true, because it sounds fatal. It's a bronchial virus that hits late at night. The child can't get any oxygen. Every time she inhales she sounds like a seal barking. There's no air getting in there.

I have a book here—*Dr. Heimlich's Home Guide to Emergency Medical Situations*—which says, "Because a child with croup is likely to be terrified at his breathing difficulty, it is essential for you to be calm yourself."

We would take Maggie into the bathroom and

run the hot shower to make steam for her to breathe. I sang her a made-up song called "Little Spudge-Face" to soothe her. One time when her breathing still didn't improve she got taken to the hospital in a fire engine, and they gave her some oxygen. I tried some myself.

She outgrew the croup when she was three, but you can't outgrow accidents. There are a lot of ways for kids to get hurt. They can burn, take poison, pull down a bookcase, have a TV fall on them during an earthquake or stick a fork in a light socket. They can fall, get stabbed, hit their heads or roll down the stairs and out the door, into the street and under a car.

Abby worried too, but she took a more practical, day-by-day attitude toward Maggie. My fear came in waves.

It was my showy concern for Maggie's safety that finally resulted in my big break.

I was at the Dogpark with her one day when she was about two. The Dogpark was a rectangular field two miles up Laguna Canyon, an acre or so of flatland at the foot of a hill. It had a chain fence on three sides and thick brush on the fourth, and you could unleash your dog there to run around. On a Saturday you'd find maybe fifty dogs there, from throughout Orange County, chasing one another. Surprisingly, they got along well; I saw a few spats, but never a real fight. People with killers weren't encouraged to bring them by.

We didn't have a dog, because we didn't have a yard, but Maggie wanted more than anything to visit the Dogpark. She'd go anywhere to see an animal. Abby thought it would be okay, and other people told me it would be okay, so one day I took her.

It was a sunny Saturday afternoon and the park was crowded. There were dachshunds, beagles, Rottweilers, setters, retrievers, cockers, a samoyed, a keeshond, some mutts and one beast of some kind as big as a card table. Most of the owners stood in little clumps. A couple of male owners threw tennis balls for their dogs to chase and called out commands that were generally ignored, what with all the socializing.

When Maggie came through the gate, she acted exactly like all the dogs did; she started running. I yelled after her not to run because it might excite some of the dogs, and she listened for a second, but then she'd run again. Great hounds would bound up to her and veer off, or they'd stop and sniff her. I didn't like it. I barked at the dogs I thought were aggressive. I picked her up to carry her on my shoulders, which she usually liked, but she squirmed and made herself boneless so I let her down for a moment. "Stay by me, then," I said. "If one comes up too hard, don't run. Stand still. Turn toward me."

A guy in a cloth cap watched us while we meandered around the park. For a while, every time a dog came up to us, I picked Maggie up and didn't let her down until the animal had proved itself docile. So she was yo-yoing quite a bit, and this apparently caught the guy's attention.

He came over to us. Most of the people at the park were in T-shirts and shorts, but he wore a button shirt and slacks. You couldn't get his age; most of him looked no more than thirty or so, but his mustache was white. He reached us as I was singing "Little Spudge-Face," the little song to Maggie that I'd made up when she had the croup. "Spudge" rhymes with "budge." It went like this:

> Little Spudge-Face is my name
> I'm a little spudge-face, yes I am
> And everybody knows my name
> They call me Little Spudge-Face

I won't claim greatness for the lyric, although the tune is catchy. I don't even know what a "spudge" is, except that when Maggie cried, her features would condense into a form that called the word to mind. We had a couple names for Maggie that weren't words, like Spudge and Widger. I'm not going to pretend we didn't.

Anyway, this gentleman approached as I finished singing. I put Maggie down so she could pet the keeshond, who was okay.

"You keep a good eye on her," said the guy.

"Well," I said, "she doesn't know what can happen."

"Got that right." He nodded, looking over the park. "And not just here. In developed countries, accidents kill and injure more kids than any disease. Babies crawl around the house like soldiers on a beachhead, in the same kind of jeopardy. On the floor—tacks, nails, pins. Ahead, sockets. Under the sink, poison. And if they pull themselves up, sharp-cornered furniture, TV sets to put their heads through. That's before they even get outside. Life is a battlefield. To survive it, they need protection."

I couldn't figure him out. He sounded part like me, part like a public service announcement, and a bit like one of those old-time gangsters who used to warn the shopkeeper about all the things that could happen to his inventory.

"You want me to pay protection for my kid?"

He looked genuinely shocked.

"*No*. I want to congratulate you. You're one of the few parents I've seen with even that much"— he held two fingers close together—"of the passion that I have on this issue. Child safety is a crusade with me. Elston Petty." He stuck out his hand, and I took it.

"I have a daughter of my own," he said. "That's why I'm forming a company dedicated to the highest tech in affordable child safety."

"Oh," I said. "Well, I'm for that. Sometimes I think Maggie oughta have a helmet just for walking around."

Petty beamed.

"You're my kind of people, Mr. . . ."

"A. J. Fleger."

He shook my hand again.

"What was that song you were singing?" he asked.

"Huh? Oh, nothing. Just some nonsense."

"What were the words?"

"Well . . ." I was embarrassed.

"Really, I'd like to hear it again, if you don't mind."

"Well, I don't *mind* . . ."

I got a firmer grasp on Maggie, and reprised

the tune. It was the first time I could recall ever being asked to sing, and I confess I was thrown off a little bit; I started in too low, which cost me later when I had to sell it on the last "They call me Little Spudge-Face" line. But Petty seemed pleased anyway.

"What is 'spudge,' a pet name?"

"Uh-huh."

"I've had a thought."

Gesturing for us to follow, he walked Maggie and me over to the thick brush at the foot of the hill, where some other dogs were sniffing around.

"I need a level head," he said, "a self-starter, with ambition, but someone who keeps himself free of folie de grandeur."

"I'm sorry?" I said.

"Delusions of grandeur."

"Oh, well, I don't think I have those."

"We're only here for a speck of time—A.J.?" I nodded and he went on. "We have to make a mark while we can. You do that by winning, and if you work for me you'll win. *I'm* going to win. Do you know why?"

He was standing in front of a large outgrowth of brush, and for a second I thought he was going to whip back the branches and show me some kind of complicated weapon.

"Because I have the vision to go with the passion. A vision of a world where every child wears a safety suit whose family can afford one. Your little girl, and my little girls, and all the other little girls are in my mind's eye throughout my day. I never lose sight of them."

"Little boys too, right?" I asked.

He nodded. "How about you? How do you feel about the world your little spudge-face is going out into?"

"Well, I'll tell you—Elston?" He nodded again. "It scares me. I'd like to keep her in a Kleenex box until she's forty."

"Kleenex box," he repeated.

"Well, I'm exaggerating."

"Yes, but the principle. Soft packing. You and I are on the same page."

And that was the start, there at the Laguna Beach Dogpark, of the Little Spudge-Face Baby Safety Company. I knew nothing at the time of entrepreneurial America, but Elston Petty came to personify it for me. His zeal, his vision, his mania, you might say, for child safety had led him to the field of mass-produced protective toddler gear, but until he met me, he hadn't found what he called the company sound.

Inside of a week we were hammering out the details of his acquisition of the little spudge-face name and song. I took $1,500, which Abby said made one of us a chump. Elston graciously suggested Maggie play herself, the original Little Spudge-Face, in the company's first local commercials; it was my suggestion that Abby record the Spudge-Face song to go with it. We also hammered out my title. Elston wanted me on the ground floor with him.

People say the American Dream is a failure or a fraud, but I didn't think so after I met Elston Petty. Suddenly, after years of drift, I was assistant vice president of marketing in a field I'd never heard of. Not only that, we were making products that were good for people. I felt the Little Spudge-Face Helmet and the Little Spudge-Face Visor were long overdue.

By 1994 Elston had leased a headquarters office with a production annex in Newport Beach, near Fashion Island, and the helmet and visor were on the market. Maggie, along with Elston's daughter Bruyana, had worn the equipment in the first commercial, to Abby's voice-over of the Spudge-Face jingle. And I was in my office, looking over the specs for the first full-body Spudge-Face Safety Suit.

I felt guilty about it sometimes. My life had turned around from the moment I went with Sterling to the Public Setback Support meeting. So had his, only the direction had been different. He was doing what he was meant to do, but he wasn't making what he needed to make, and I was no longer around to encourage him. Where Sterling was concerned, I had become one of those guys who tell you what you should do but aren't there to hold your coat while you do it.

Then in October of '94, he got back on network TV, and taking all the results into consideration I'd have to say it didn't go as well as it did the first time.

Earlier that year, on May 24, a man later identified as Lester Bogle had walked into the Mission Vista Public Library in San Juan Capistrano. About a dozen other people were in the library that day. Bogle made his way to the middle of the adult nonfiction section, produced a Belgian assault rifle from underneath a camouflage jacket and began firing from the hip, turning once around to spray bullets in a circle from nonfiction to fiction to the magazine area, the checkout desk, the computer well and the large-print section, coming to a stop back in nonfiction, E–G. He killed restaurateur Garland Bernard of San Clemente and wounded five others, including Carole Neale, the librarian. Then he walked past the checkout counter and out the front door, trotted to a dirty old Chevy pickup and drove away.

Bogle was still at large that fall, when his crime was dramatized on the prime-time reality show "Open Cases." That's the one that ends each week with the guy saying, "And this is still . . . an Open Case." Sterling was cast as Bogle. It was national exposure, but of course it was taped, not live, and Sterling found the role skeletal and confining.

"Basically, reality programming is just hitting marks," he told me on the phone a week before the show aired. "You go in and do what they say the guy did. You can't make any choices of your own. I got the part because I look like a typical killer in a baseball cap and a plaid shirt."

"Why did the guy do it?" I asked. "Why spray a library?"

"Apparently someone there called him a white-trash dysfunctional."

"They'll know better next time."

"Hey," said Sterling. "I'm not the guy, okay? It's a job. They need to *catch* the guy. This is a civic duty performance."

"Well, Maggie's not watching Uncle Sterling in this one."

"Hell, no. I'm not watching it either."

Abby and I tuned in, though, when "Open Cases" aired a few days before Halloween. Sterling was suitably repellent in the recreated library, impassively blasting away at bookshelves and bookworms alike.

"I don't know why they call the case open," said Abby, grimacing. "It's pretty clear who did it."

"The open part is where the guy is," I said.

They showed a 1-800 number you could call if you knew the whereabouts of Lester Bogle. And they showed an old photograph of a scraggly, unshaven, standard-issue American homicidal maniac.

After the show, I called Sterling and left congratulations on the machine at his new apartment in Fullerton. Then I don't remember anything else until we got a call from him at 2 A.M.

"Didn't you get my message?" I asked him.

"Yeah." He sounded disgruntled. "I got it."

"Well, what's up? It's late."

"I'm in Orange County Jail."

I was shocked. Neither of us had ever spent time in a major jail.

"*Why?*" I asked.

"My new neighbors called the fucking toll-free number and turned me in," he said bitterly.

"Jeez," I said. "You fooled your own neighbors."

"Yeah, well, I've had training, you know."

"Didn't you tell the cops who you were?"

"Yeah, but I did it in such a way that they arrested me anyhow. I'd appreciate it, Age"—he lowered his voice—"if you could please get here real soon."

CHAPTER EIGHT

Sterling asked me to call Toni Boyce so she and I could co-identify him. We weren't sure how many people it would take to extricate him from the Orange County Jail, a big, grim building on Flower Street in Santa Ana.

Beyond having to identify him, I also had to bail him out, because he'd made a disturbance when the police arrived at his apartment. Fortunately they only make you pay ten percent of the bail up front, and there were several bondsmen in the neighborhood.

The procedure took until late morning. Toni and I waited for Sterling in a civilian outer area of the jail. She said she hadn't seen much of him since he'd left Dittmer's and moved to the cheaper apartment in Fullerton.

"I would point out," she said to me, "that we

never had to do this when he was a job counselor."

He finally emerged, in a gray sweatshirt and jeans, moving as if achey and sore. His hair and skin were oily and he had a two-day beard. He gave a little embarrassed smile and said, "Each dawn I die."

He was eager to leave the building, so we exited to the large front lawn area. I suggested brunch, and Toni asked Sterling where he wanted to eat.

"Outdoors," he said, breathing deeply. "The air in there is unbelievable. People don't mention it enough. It's like it must have been in the first submarine."

He rode with Toni as she followed me to Little Spudge-Face headquarters in Newport Beach. It's a glass-and-marble building, seven stories. We've got space on the fifth. There's a ground-floor café, with little iron tables out front on the sidewalk. We parked in the lot and went and sat down at one of them.

Sterling seemed self-conscious, sitting out there among all the office workers in their skirts and white shirts. He kept swiping at the sweat and oil on his face with paper napkins. He took a look at his reflection in the café window, then adjusted his chair and turned his back on himself.

He said, "I looked in a storefront window on our way to the car, and you know what I saw, walking along? I saw a ragged, washed-up bum." He shook his head. "Turned out to be a guy in the store going the same direction, but it could've been me, way I'm going."

He leaned forward earnestly to tell us about jail.

"This overcrowding is a disgrace. After I went through the shower and they gave me my clothes and my pallet, they put me in a long cell with forty-five other guys. Bunks on one side, a little aisle on the other that goes to the john. The only spot to put my pallet was right in front of the latrine. I tried it for a minute. Everybody's stepping over me, going in and out. I was a speed bump.

"So I sat back against the wall, next to this giant tattooed guy. He goes, 'What are you in for?' They really say that. I said, 'Well, it's a mistake, I'm not the guy.' He says 'Me neither.' Says he's in for aggravated murder. Aggravated. I said, 'I don't think I ever heard of that.' He says, 'It's murder with extra shit.'"

Sterling shook his head again.

"I wondered if he was gonna rape me before or after he killed me. I was so scared, I just acted dull and sleepy. I said, 'This effin' HIV, you don't have any energy.'"

He ordered a roast beef sandwich on sourdough with extra mayonnaise. "In jail they have this stringy stuff you can't look at," he said. "Picture a restaurant where all the waiters and the maître d' are going to club you if you send it back. The guards hate us."

I watched him rip open a bag of Sun Chips.

"Well, it's flattering though, isn't it?" I said.

Sterling and Toni both stared at me.

"I mean, it proves you were good, if they thought you were Lester Bogle."

Sterling sniffed.

"Any derelict could have done as well. Lester Bogle looks like all the other criminals on 'Open Cases,' and now that I'm older and poorer, I do too."

He had a point. It was hard to see the high school graduation picture in Sterling, there at the café.

"Now's the time to stop, hon," said Toni. "This isn't what you went back into acting for. If you apologize to Nathan and promise you'll stick with it this time, maybe you can get your job back."

Sterling didn't respond right away. Instead, he futzed around with the newspaper I'd brought, flipping through the pages.

Suddenly he stopped and leaned forward.

"Oh, no," he said.

I noticed he was looking at the obituaries and said, "Oh, yeah. Burt Lancaster died."

"This is worse," said Sterling, and spun the paper around so I could see the page he was looking at.

It was a short, seven-paragraph obituary on the bottom of page 34 of the *Times* for Wednesday, October 26. The subject was sixty-six-year-old actor Robert Lansing, who had died of cancer in New York.

"Can you believe that?" said Sterling in indignant despair. "Look at that rickety picture. From 1966. And look at that piddling writeup."

Actually it was a respectful little summary of Lansing's career. It was headed "Robert Lansing; Starred in Hit 1960s TV Series."

The last paragraph went as follows:

But Lansing is probably best remembered as the authoritarian Brig. Gen. Frank Savage in "12 O'Clock High." The ABC drama series about World War II bomber pilots aired from Sept. 18, 1964, through Jan. 13, 1967. Lansing's character died at the beginning of the second season.

By the time I finished reading, Sterling was back from the newsstand in the building lobby with copies of *Variety* and *The Hollywood Reporter*.

"Cancer," I said as he searched through them. "Sixty-six. I wonder if that'll be us. We inhaled the same way he did."

"This is a goddamn joke," said Sterling. "He's page six, no picture in the *Reporter* and *nothing* in *Variety*."

"Maybe it'll be in there tomorrow."

Sterling stabbed his finger at the picture in the *L.A. Times*.

"This guy did *Suddenly, Last Summer* on Broadway and he should've been in the movie, but they gave it to Montgomery Clift. Then he got replaced in '12 O'Clock High' because they said he couldn't bring in the young audience. We were a young audience, weren't we? This guy *never* got the recognition he deserved. What about the 'Twilight Zone' where he was the astronaut who took himself out of suspended animation so he'd age at the same rate as Mariette Hartley?"

"People are looking," murmured Toni.

"Okay," said Sterling. "He didn't do much comedy. But he showed how to behave under pressure. He projected intelligence. If I'd thought of him during the Manson bit, I never would've blown that line."

He sat for a moment, dazed.

"I didn't even know he was *sick*. I would've written . . . I saw him on 'Kung Fu: The Legend Continues' the other night and he looked *fine*. I just thought, What's he doing in *this* crap?"

"Everybody can hear you," said Toni.

"They should," said Sterling, rising with the *Times* obit in his hand and turning to the other lunchers. "Robert Lansing died," he announced.

This declaration met with no uproar.

Sterling stepped to the nearest table.

"Do you know who this is?" he said, shoving the paper at the guy sitting there.

The man leaned his head back to look down his nose. "Should I?"

"If you know who Robert Stack is, you should know who this is," said Sterling.

"*Isn't* it Robert Stack?"

"*No*. Can't you read?"

"I can read," said the guy with some menace, starting to get up. Then he took a closer look at Sterling and reconsidered.

"He's not Robert Conrad, Robert Wagner, Robert Vaughn or Bob Crane," said Sterling, now at another table, at which two portly guys sat. "You guys are about my age. You ever watch TV? This guy was one of the best actors on TV when we were growing up. He could be a good guy or a bad guy. He was one of our first images of competent adulthood."

"He was on 'The Equalizer,' " remarked one, looking at the photo.

"Damn right. And he was 'The Man Who Never Was' too, but nobody remembers that."

"You a relative of this guy?" asked the other customer at the table.

"I wouldn't know," said Sterling.

"Well, what's your point?"

"My point," said Sterling, waving the newspaper for the edification of the rest of the café, "is that this is not sufficient recognition for this man. He's on page thirty-four."

"He got a picture," observed a nearby woman, pointing at the flanking obit on the page. "He got more than Carl Sharsmith"—she squinted—"naturalist at Yosemite Park."

"Carl Sharsmith didn't play Gary Seven on 'Star Trek,' " said Sterling.

"That's not in here," said her male companion, as the owner of the café came outside to see what the noise was about. "How do you know all this shit?"

"Shit?" said Sterling.

"Hey," said the owner.

"It was TV, big deal," said the guy at the table.

"The man had style," said Sterling. "That's shit?"

"I don't allow that language," said the owner.

"He's okay," I said to the owner, taking Sterling by the arm. "He's distraught."

Sterling turned to me, stricken.

"He was on every tube in America. And this isn't fifty years ago. This is in living memory. I mean, what's the use? Nobody cares. They don't even know who he *was*."

"Oh, I do," said a woman sitting alone at a far table. She nodded emphatically. "In 'The Twilight Zone,' he was an astronaut. He took himself out of suspended animation on his long space flight so he'd get old along with Mariette Hartley back on earth. But she froze herself while he was in space, so when he came back, she was still young, but he was old. It was sad. I cried. I think I was about eight."

Sterling stared at this woman. She was pretty, I thought, in a grown-up, crinkly, kind of tired or sleepy way, like someone who got up early to get ready for work. She had a nice suit on, and she had brown hair with some strands of gray in it.

Sterling walked toward her, slowly. She showed traces of worry, and I didn't blame her. He didn't look altogether sane or solvent.

When he got to the woman's table, he looked down at her and said, "Maybe he lived so we could meet."

Toni Boyce said, "That's it," put money on the table for her decaf, and got up, slinging her bag over her shoulder. To me she said, "Better if he'd missed the swimming pool."

Sterling looked exalted as I drove him to his apartment. He was still sad about Robert Lansing, but he felt vindicated in his life's ambition.

"It's not being famous. Nobody stays famous.

But your work can be remembered by a stranger. That's what matters."

"Shows how people see things differently," I said. "When I'm gone, I don't care if people sit around talking about me or not."

"Well, you're right to feel that way," said Sterling cryptically.

He was all aflame over Valerie Fassero, the woman from the café. She was a divorcée who worked for a company in our building. Sterling said he admired her nerve. I said I did too.

"It took guts for her to talk to you, way you looked."

"I meant," he said patiently, "that most people won't admit to being affected by old television."

Sterling now lived on the ground floor of a two-story building in a slightly rundown section of Fullerton. He was looking forward to canvassing his neighbors to find out which one of them had turned him in. He was full of energy all of a sudden. It was remarkable what this woman had done for him. He got onto the subject of destiny—his, Robert Lansing's and Valerie's—and stayed on it until we entered the apartment and were met, inside the door, with a powerful aroma. It seemed to be about twenty percent burning grease and eighty percent the scent that emanates from a guy who doesn't worry about how he smells.

"You oughta air this place out," I said.

"No, wait," muttered Sterling. He paused for a moment, sniffing. Then he quietly took the phone off the little table by the door, put the phone on the floor and carried the table with him to the kitchen.

The smell in there was coming from a thin rib-eye steak on the front burner and the man frying it. He was short and stout, with thin, silky blond hair, and he wore an old, stained trenchcoat over a T-shirt and jeans. When he smiled at Sterling, the corners of his upper lip curved downward.

"Your mama wants ya," he said.

Days later, Sterling asked me how he looked when he was told his mother wanted him. It was a typical actor's question. He wanted to file his reaction for study. I couldn't answer him because I didn't know. I was staring at his guest.

His hair was dirtier than Sterling's, and he ate his steak right out of the pan, holding it up with a fork and spinning it with each bite until the remainder was small enough to stuff into his mouth.

"She saw you on TV," he said during this process, "and we watched the names at the end. Then we looked in all the phone books till we found you." He gestured at the window. "Your back slider's broken."

He put the fork down and rubbed his face thoroughly with a paper towel.

"Leavin' on Track 29," he said.

I was against accompanying this guy anywhere, but he fascinated Sterling. I wound up joining the two of them in a little old yellow Toyota. Our driver didn't want me, but I insisted. I didn't want Sterling going off with him alone.

The car had been in at least one accident. The front passenger door wouldn't close. "You have to hold it shut," the guy told Sterling. I sat in the back, with some fast-food wrappers and some old clothes.

Our driver was smug. He chortled periodically, glancing at Sterling, and in the rear-view mirror at me. He drove us down the 5 all the way to San Juan Capistrano. He liked country music on the radio, and sang along with it. At first I thought he was doing harmony, but he was trying to do the tune.

San Juan Capistrano is twenty minutes south of Laguna and five minutes inland. It's famous for its old mission and the swallows that come back every year. It has a pretty little downtown area. A couple of the residential neighborhoods are chipped and peeling, though, and it was to one of these that our guide drove us. He parked in the driveway of a small bungalow with a patchy little yard. The house was cracked stucco. He took us in the back door, through a dark kitchen and into a darker living room.

The TV was on, to an old black-and-white "Perry Mason." I remember because Jeremy Slate was the defendant and he's one of Sterling's old favorites.

"I just can't watch that O.J. anymore," said the woman on the couch. "I'd rather watch one that ends in an hour."

She was portly, with thick forearms. She had gray hair in tight, frizzy curls. She wore a print dress and glasses. She overpowered the couch.

Sterling's expression as he looked down at the woman was apprehensive. Her look back at him, as she labored to her feet, was sunny and affectionate. I guess maternal. She hugged him while he looked helplessly at me, hands at his sides. Then she leaned back and looked up at his face ecstatically.

"There it is!" she boomed at our chauffeur, who was standing over by the kitchen door. She pointed up at Sterling's head. "There's that chin. Sharp as a hoe. And there's that ear. No lobe. Just goes directly into his head. All your daddy's family's ears go like that. My Big Boy Blue. My Big Beautiful Boy Blue."

Sterling stared down at her.

"Do you think you're my mother?" he asked.

"Oh, you can't see it because you take after your dad," she said. "But I'm your mama and I always have been and I always will be, and you're my Vinnie, and I'll say this: I never thought you'd live, I couldn't afford, I couldn't take care of you, otherwise I'd never've given you up, and you can ask Denny." Tears sprang into her eyes. "Chicago Child Care Association. I almost died. I *thought* I'd die, I *wanted* to die. Say you remember me, sweetie. Say you do. Say you do. Say, 'I remember you, Mama.' "

Sterling tilted his head dubiously.

"Uh—"

"*Dixie!*" she screamed. Sterling and I recoiled. "*Dixie!*"

She went to a sliding screen door leading into the backyard and bellowed "*Dixie!*" again.

"You get in here this *minute*!" she yelled. A tubby little dachshund came in as she opened the door. "You were just supposed to do poop and a potty," she told him. He waddled over to smell our feet.

Our chauffeur moved to turn off the TV but she said, "Leave it on. We like it for company."

Sterling was peering at her in doubt and consternation. She didn't look like him. Of course they were different sexes and twenty-five or so years apart, but she was different anyway, with thinner lips and blueish, watery eyes and a dissimilar shape to her head. I couldn't see that Sterling and this woman had the same anything, although they were both large.

I noticed a few photographs on a mantel shelf and went over to look at them. Sterling and the woman and her dog followed me.

"There, you can see in that one," she said, pointing at a faded Polaroid of a man with a mustache squinting into the sun. "See the Bogle chin? And here—here's all of us, your daddy, Lester and me. You look at the men and you can see you're a Bogle."

Sterling stared at them.

"Lester's mad at Vinnie, isn't he, Dixie?" said the woman to her dog, picking him up and squeezing him in her arms until he yelped. "About that show. But I'm not mad," she snuggled up next to Sterling, "because I saw my Boy Blue on that show. My Bibbity Bobbity Blue."

There was an old snapshot of a skinny teenager—young Lester Bogle—striking a bodybuilder's stance on a small lawn in front of a white clapboard house. Beside it was a more recent pose, in which Lester wore a mustache and a New Orleans Saints cap. He looked a lot grimmer in the later picture, standing in a room somewhere, looking down at the photographer.

"He hated how you did him on that show," Mrs. Bogle went on. "You made him out a monster. You know, people can change. It takes some of us longer to get our lives together."

Sterling looked down at her and said, distinctly, "I don't know you."

"Well, you got your daddy's memory," she said. "Got his voice too. He was wonderful with regional accents. But when the pressure was on, his memory failed him."

We looked at the first picture again, the one of the squinting man. He did resemble Sterling, in build and facial shape, but there was no stunning resemblance.

"Your name," she said, "is Vincent Charles Bogle. You were so sick, and your father was incarcerated in Illinois, and you had asthma, and the worst case of cradle cap—bend over a minute. Come here."

She pulled Sterling's head down and pawed briefly through his hair, searching the scalp.

"Well, you outgrew it," she said. "Hope you outgrew the rash on your hoosie."

Sterling flinched and backed away as Mrs. Bogle snickered.

"We won't look. We won't embarrass him. But, honey, honestly, I had no way to take care of you. And I have lived with it all these years, and you have no idea how hard that was." She shook her head and her lip quivered. "Does he, Dixie? He doesn't know, does he?"

She turned away from us and rummaged through a dresser drawer. Sterling couldn't take his eyes off her. Denny smirked at us all from the kitchen doorway. Mrs. Bogle finally turned triumphantly.

"*Here* he is."

She held out a small, square black-and-white photograph with serrated edges. It showed a little kid standing in a doorway. Pudgy face, wide eyes, high forehead, shorts with suspenders, dimpled knees. Apprehensive look.

"On your first birthday," she said. "March 3, 1955."

We stared at it. It could've been him, but it also could've been somebody else. I found it inconclusive. Sterling, however, was shaken.

"Good God," he said.

"Do you remember that apartment?" she asked.

"No."

"Just like your daddy," she said.

"How could I remember? I was *one.*"

"You know why Lester's really mad?" she asked, holding the photo up, closer to Sterling's face. "He's disappointed. He's hurt that his own *brother* would make him out to be a mad killer."

Sterling was incredulous.

"First off," he said, "I never heard of Lester before I took the part. And second, he shot up a *library.*"

"Not the children's section," Mother Bogle amended. "Lester would never hurt a child."

Sterling blinked, wandered over to the couch,

sat down and began watching Jeremy Slate on "Perry Mason."

"And you are . . . ?" said Mother Bogle to me.

"I'm his brother," I said firmly. "Adlai Fleger."

"Well, I'm sure you feel you are, but blood tells the tale. I'm Loretta." She went to sit beside Sterling. "Honey, do you forgive me for letting you go? If your father hadn't been in jail, or if you hadn't been so sick . . ."

"Oh, well," said Sterling.

"Are you sure, honey? Because I could die happy if you forgave— Well, not *happy*. There's one other thing we've *got* to do and that's get Lester out of the country. And you should help because it's your fault he can't even go to the store. Izza wizza Vinnie's fault," she said, nuzzling Dixie, who struggled in her grip.

Sterling stared at her in bewilderment. He'd been up all night in jail, and Robert Lansing had died, and now this.

"Are you my mother?" he asked, like the little bird in the story I used to read Maggie.

The woman patted her stomach complacently.

"Excuse me," I said, stepping forward. "I'm sure you see yourself as his mom and all, but even if you are, which *I* don't believe, you haven't been around lately, and he and I already have a mother and she's been sufficient, so—"

"We have to take Lester his doughnuts," said Mother Bogle, pulling Sterling up from the couch. "Come on, honey. TV later."

Sterling followed her. He looked at me, and I could see it. He believed her. I couldn't figure it out.

To me, she was just a deluded old relic of the type that Shelley Winters occasionally plays. But maybe there was something about her that struck only him—something about her voice, or her smell, or her eyes. Maybe I would know you.

CHAPTER NINE

They say you can't choose your relatives, and in Sterling's case, that maxim was driven home with unusual force at the age of forty.

After all those years as Sterling Fleger, he was now told that he was Vincent Charles Bogle, son of Joe and Loretta, given up to the Chicago Child Care Association at the age of eighteen months in late 1955.

Daddy Joe was a gifted but unlucky confidence man from whom, Mrs. Bogle claimed, Sterling inherited his voice and acting ability. Joe did two kinds of Englishman ("upper and lower"), a New Yorker, a hick, a white South African and, of course, a Midwesterner, which is what he was. His flaw was a tendency to confuse his aliases and answer to the wrong name at a crucial time. Joe Bogle had never otherwise shown the effects of the stress of his profession, but had bottled it up and eventually "blown his top," dying of a stroke at fifty-eight. "But I'm looking at him again, right this second," said Loretta Bogle, snuggling up close to Sterling in the back seat of Denny's car.

Denny, our driver, was a kind of foster Bogle; he had grown up next door to the family in downstate Illinois. His most noteworthy attribute was that he was from the future.

"Denny comes from 2062," said Mrs. Bogle.

"Really," said Sterling after a moment.

"He knows what's going to happen to all of us."

Well, who doesn't, I thought. But Denny smiled at the windshield as if he had detailed information.

"How'd you get here?" I asked him finally.

"Same way as Kang the Conqueror," he said. "Look it up."

Mrs. Bogle whispered to Sterling, "We go along. Makes him feel useful."

I heard her, so Denny had to hear her too, but he didn't show it.

He drove us to a biker saloon in the center of the San Juan Capistrano business district. We stayed in the car while Denny consulted someone inside, then rejoined us on the street.

"Okay," he said.

He got back in the driver's seat and I held the right front door shut while he drove us through residential streets until he was satisfied with the rearview mirror. Then he drove to the ocean, to Dana Point.

Dana Point Harbor consists of several piers,

restaurants, shops, and a huge and beautiful collection of sailing vessels, all in their slips, I believe
they're called. We parked and walked to the end of
one pier, where a man sat in the sunlight, wearing
a fishing hat and sunglasses and carrying a rod.

Lester Bogle had shaved and cut his hair. He
wore a raggedy sport coat with thin chocolate stripes
and an orange-and-black shirt with the tail exposed.
He looked like a neon sign with a couple bulbs
burned out, but he had succeeded in distancing himself from his TV picture. He didn't move when we
came up.

"Hi, lamb," said Loretta Bogle. "Got your
doughnuts. Brought you a surprise too."

He looked up—a skinny-faced, pockmarked
guy of thirty-five or so, with one side of his tanned
face screwed up against the sun. I was disheartened
to see that he squinched up his face the same way
Sterling squinched his. He flicked a look at me, then
fixed his gaze on Sterling.

"Hollywood," he said. "Do you *ever* get it
right?"

He stood up—he was Sterling's height—and
addressed him without preamble, as though resum-
ing an argument begun earlier in the day.

"The way you did me, everybody thinks I'm
crazy," he said. "I might just as well go ahead and
be a shit *now*."

"Keep your voice down, honey," said his
mother.

Lester gave a pained look at a couple of tourists
strolling past.

"I was in the desert," he said, more confidentially. "Now I can't stay there, I can't stay here. You made me a man without a country."

Sterling peered at him, searching for evidence of a relationship. To me they looked similar, but not strikingly so except for the squinch. Of course, I didn't *want* to see anything.

"Look how he looks at me," said Lester. "Like I'm from the moon. That's the way he did me too. What was that walk?" He stalked stiff-legged down the pier and back, in exaggerated imitation of Sterling's portrayal. "*Night of the Living Dead*? And the talk through the nose. Why didn't you just go ahead and drool?"

As he ended his parody, he took notice of me for the first time.

"Who's this?" he demanded.

"I'm his brother," I said.

"He's not blood. He shouldn't be here," said Lester flatly.

I was in agreement. I could see Lester didn't like me. And he lacked one of the reasons most people have not to kill those they dislike—namely, that they haven't killed anyone before.

"Why'n'tcha get your ass out of here," Lester suggested to me.

"Why don't we both?" I asked Sterling.

"Just a minute," said Mrs. Bogle. "We want Vinnie to pretend to be Lester long enough for Lester to go through to Tijuana."

Sterling continued squinting bleakly at Lester.

"It's a family obligation, sweetie," Mrs. Bogle told him. "And you haven't been doing yours."

"You dragged our whole name through the

mud on that show," said Lester. "Especially mine."

That last remark hit Sterling funny. He snorted once.

"How'd you like the way I shot the women?" he said.

Lester's face got all bony and drained. His lips disappeared and his eyes got buggy. He breathed through his nose.

"So you're ashamed of me," he said.

Sterling laughed suddenly, an involuntary bark. Lester took it bad.

"Well, fuck you, man, just fuckin' fuck you," he said. He shot both hands at Sterling's chest. Sterling brought his hands up and pushed Lester's arms apart. They did that two or three more times and then Mrs. Bogle stepped between them.

"Boys!" she demanded.

Lester and Sterling subsided. Lester walked away down the pier and looked at the gulls. Then he turned and came back to face Sterling.

"Where were you?" he inquired. "How much fuckin' guidance did you ever provide?"

"You need somebody to tell you not to shoot up a library?" asked Sterling.

"Oh, yeah, it's so bad 'cause it was the library. 'Shhhhhhh . . .' I wasn't in there two minutes, this bitch comes over to sweep me out the door."

"That's why you did it?"

"Hey, I don't have to give you a reason for everything I do."

Lester glared at a nearby sailboat, remembering.

"Like they'd ever let me on that show to tell

my side. I was having a bad time," he said heavily. He suddenly seemed near tears. "Construction totally flattened out . . . State went to hell as soon as we got out here . . . I came in to sit for a minute and this *bean* won't get out of the chair, and next thing I know I got all these people lookin' at me like I'm parrot shit. Well, I don't take that, that's all. I'm sorry. There's too much disrespect."

I glanced at Mother Bogle during this conversation, but saw no trace of the "Where did I go wrong?" attitude. I wondered if she'd read stories to Lester when he was a boy, and what stories they were if she did. Maybe they were about the Old South. People in that culture were very sensitive to perceived insults.

"I was very quiet," continued Lester. "I told this woman to get out of my face. Then the mayor of Fagtown comes up and says I'm what's wrong with America! In front of everybody. Tell you what," Lester said, pointing a finger at Sterling's chest. "The guy who said that, *he* was what's wrong with America."

"Well, then America must be all better now," said Sterling, "because you *killed* him."

"You wanta let me finish? Him and the atheist welfare government abortionists and the liberal Jew dykes in the *library* are what's wrong with America. When I see what's on TV, it makes me sick."

Lester went on for a few moments with some radio call-in material. Sterling looked out at the boats, breathing heavily.

I believe I know what he was thinking. For years you have one family, then suddenly you're confronted by a nightmare replacement set. When we were in our teens, we never imagined that our mystery relatives could be worse than our present ones. You just don't fantasize in that direction.

I hadn't accepted the Bogle premise yet, but Sterling had. You could see it from the way he stood. He was a sinking ship, there on the pier. What with the long night, the hot sun, the photographs, the resemblances, and that indefinable reminiscent aura Loretta Bogle seemed to give off, Sterling was sure it was true. He was disappearing beneath the foam, right before me.

After a few more comments on civics, Lester veered to another subject.

"I'll tell you something else," he said. "I'm myself. Dad was always Earl So-and-So or Joey Ricca or Gomer Pyle. By the time he died he didn't know who the fuck he was. You're like that too, aren't ya? Big actor. Well, I'm Lester Bogle. They don't like it they can eat it."

"Lester's not what's wrong with America," said Mrs. Bogle. "The way you did him on TV, you made him seem like What's-his-name, Helter Skelter. And he's not. He has wonderful qualities. You never saw him growing up. He's loyal. He can fix anything. His problem is he won't moderate his diet"—at this point Lester sighed and closed his eyes—"and he eats and drinks things he's allergic to. He also reacts violently to synthetic perfume, which this library woman was covered with. His ex-wife wore the same scent. He's just now coming out of it."

"Reacts violently, does he," commented Sterling.

"Oh, like you never wanted to take out a roomful of assholes," said Lester.

Sterling regarded him for a moment. Then he sat down on a piling and gently rubbed his eyelids. He looked exhausted.

"Are you gonna help us, honey?" asked Mrs. Bogle. "Help your brother? Help your mama?"

I walked over to Sterling.

"These are not your people," I muttered.

"Yeah, they are," he said.

I stared at him. He was a mess. He looked beaten and bloodless.

Then Lester came to the rescue.

"Hey, you help me out, bro," he said, "or else."

I believe that was one of the very few remarks that could've perked Sterling up at that point—one of Dad's old phrases. It hit Sterling like cool water. He raised his head, refreshed.

"Or else what?" he asked curiously. "Oh, wait. I get it: Or *else*. Whoa. Okay. Put it like that . . . I'll do it. I'll help you. But first, just do one thing for me, okay? Blow me. Right here. A little hummer. Kinda get me off to a good start."

Mrs. Bogle drew back, offended.

"Now that was uncalled for," she said. "Don't you do it, Lester."

"You're funny," Lester told Sterling.

"You're not gonna?" asked Sterling.

"You'll see what I do. How about if I do

him"—he gestured at me—"and his family too, how about that?"

Well, it degenerated from there. I shouldered past Denny and called Lester a name, I don't remember what, and we started punching and pushing at each other, there on the pier. He got me pretty good on the ear. He was stringy but muscular. Sterling and Denny mixed in, and Mrs. Bogle pulled at us from the outskirts. You could have gotten the lot of us on one of those daytime talk shows, no problem.

I thought we'd all end up in the water in one another's grasp, but while we surged and staggered back and forth, Denny hissed "*Strategy*" at Lester, and Mrs. Bogle grunted, "Public, public." We gradually revolved to a stop. People in the dockside restaurants were looking at us through the windows.

"They'll call the toll-free number," Denny warned Lester.

"Why? I don't look like that picture on TV anymore," said Lester.

"No, but *he* does," said Denny, indicating Sterling.

We all stood and panted at one another.

"Shit, I'm goin'," said Lester.

"Don't be mad, honey," said Mrs. Bogle.

Lester snorted and looked at Sterling.

"Vinnie this and that. I wasn't as cute as you, I wasn't as smart as you, I didn't even get as sick as you. But you aren't much. You had to play me. I'm the one who's real, not you."

He started off, then turned for a parting remark.

"Don't try to narc me," he called. "I won't be here, know what I'm sayin'? I'll get back to you."

He stumped up toward the shops and restaurants and disappeared, walking through a clump of people who stared after him. I couldn't believe he hadn't been caught, the way he called attention to himself.

After dropping Mrs. Bogle at her house, Denny drove us back to Sterling's apartment in Fullerton. He told us Lester would be in touch, and that Sterling would be wise to adjust his thinking and rally round his brother.

"What if he doesn't?" I asked.

Denny shrugged with his eyebrows.

"He might piss on your doorknob," he said.

At first I took this as a metaphor, another way of saying "rain on our parade," but Denny explained that back home in Illinois Lester had expressed his displeasure with a neighbor by urinating repeatedly on her front door until the entire lock mechanism corroded and had to be replaced.

"Or he might do like at the library," said Denny. "When I see him"—he gestured out ahead of him, in the air—"I see sudden, explosive movement."

Sterling no longer reacted to anything he heard. When we got back, he got out of Denny's car and went into his apartment without a word. I followed him inside as Denny drove away.

The first thing I had to do was call home. I got Abby and asked her to take Maggie to her mother's house.

"Why?"

"We got a thumbs way down on Sterling's performance from the original guy."

After agreeing to meet her later at the Zanes', I tracked Sterling into his kitchen, where he sat with a beer, staring at the frying pan Denny had dined out of.

"Resemblance, by itself," I told him, "means nothing. On 'The Big Valley'—remember? *You* pointed this out—Richard Long, Peter Breck and Lee Majors all looked like brothers. But were they related?"

Sterling walked past me to the living room and stood before the mirror, where he did a silent scream and made the cords on his neck stand out, as he always did. This was a form of exercise. Then he repeated most of Lester's facial expressions, one after another. He finally stopped and gazed at himself morosely.

"I'm a Bogle," he said.

He walked past me again, slumped onto the couch and stared at the TV, which was off.

"You're a Fleger," I said.

He was silent for a moment.

"I'm a Boglefleger," he said finally. "I'm a Fleeglebooger."

I sat down on his coffee table and faced him.

"Even if you are, you don't have to act like one. People don't have to be like their relatives. You're not just a Fleger or a Bogle. You're a suburbanite."

"You're lucky," he said dully. "You never found out. You never came face-to-face with your true self."

"Oh, bullshit. You're not like those people."

Sterling blinked at the TV and lethargically mimicked Mrs. Bogle.

" 'Not the children's section.' That's an indulgent mother, wouldn't you say? I bet *she* would've let me stay up past nine-thirty."

"What are you gonna do?"

He looked at his palms.

"I don't know, it's like . . . you and I were always unlimited. There weren't any boundaries to who we could be, because we didn't know of any. Now I feel like I've been classified, boxed, and stamped 'F.' I mean, that's some crew. Dad was Ward Cleaver compared to those people." He sat up straighter as a thought occurred to him. "And I'll bet I was wired to blow that line. Did you hear that part about Joe Bogle saying the wrong name? Under pressure? I'll bet if I got another chance, I'd dick it up again."

There was a solid knock on the door, and I jumped. Sterling breathed mightily through his nose, stood up, walked over and jerked the door open. When he stood aside, there was Valerie Fassero from the Robert Lansing café.

Seeing her in the doorway, I revised my opinion of her upward. She wasn't flashy, but she wore a nice suit and her hair was full and kind of swept. She looked elegant. She also looked hesitant, and that made her attractive.

"I thought we had a dinner date," she said.

For a few minutes Sterling pretended everything was normal. He welcomed her in, sat her down on the couch and offered her some Chex mix from a bowl on the table.

"These have been picked through," she observed.

"I like the wheat ones," he admitted.

He asked her about her job and listened with such wide-eyed attention that I knew he wasn't absorbing anything.

"There's not much drama in it," she said. "It's not something you want on your tombstone: 'I distributed digital remote hand-held bar-code scanners.' The only interesting thing that happened in twelve years was when some people picketed us because they said bar codes were invented by the Antichrist."

Sterling showed signs of consciousness at that.

"I had a girlfriend who said that," he said. "Lee Ann," he added to me. "Just before she left."

"Anyway," said Valerie, "that was a few years ago and ever since I've been thinking, Sure is quiet in here. I was touched by what you said at the café about Robert Lansing."

Sterling blinked, wakening.

"You were?"

They stared at each other.

"Yes," she said. "I was. I was moved. You showed me . . . feeling. You reminded me."

"Well," he said. "You did more for me than I did for you. You remembered."

"Oh, I remember them all," she said, nodding.

"You do?"

"They were my companions too. I mean, you have to have standards, but . . . the good ones."

They were talking softer, with pauses, as they looked into each other's eyes. I found myself ducking my head forward to try to pick up the words.

Sterling's eyes narrowed.

"Ever see . . . 'He and She'?" he asked quietly.

Her eyes widened.

"Oh, that's so weird. I modeled myself on Paula Prentiss! And Dick Benjamin had that great non-reaction. And Jack Cassidy. One time Dick Benjamin came home to Paula and found Jack Cassidy hiding in the closet. And Dick Benjamin said, 'I'm sure there's a good explanation for this,' and Jack Cassidy goes, 'Okay, let's hear it.' "

She laughed reminiscently, finishing with, "Ahhhh . . . They shouldn't've canceled it."

A flame lit in Sterling's eyes during this speech, but then it dimmed. He sat back and exhaled.

"You and I have no future," he muttered. "Two hours ago I wouldn't've said that."

She stared at him, mystified.

"But now you're tired?"

"Now I know who I really am," he said.

"Oh, bull," I said. To Valerie I explained, "He was up all night."

"I was in *jail*," said Sterling bitterly, rising and going to the door, "because my neighbors thought I was a Bogle."

He yanked the door open and yelled out into the dusk.

"*You were right after all, you rat bastards!*" he yelled, and slammed the door. Then he turned back to her. His shoulders slumped as he leaned back against the door.

"I'm a Bogle," he told her quietly.

I don't know when I've been so disgusted. Valerie Fassero looked to be as good a match for him as God could have made from a kit. Yet here he was, thrusting her from him with the tainted-blood sequence from *Arsenic and Old Lace*.

"What is he talking about?" she asked me.

"Oh, he met a murderer he thinks is his brother."

"Wow," she said.

Sterling stood by the phone, irresolute.

"Call the cops," I said. "We can't tell 'em where he is, but we can tell 'em where he was."

"Annnhhhhhhhh," he said, and shook his head.

"He's not your brother."

"Yeah, he is."

I got up.

"Well, he isn't mine."

As I reached the phone, Sterling rested a couple fingers gently on the earpiece. I looked up at him.

"A library?" I said. "How you gonna feel when he visits a theme park?"

Sterling chewed on the insides of his cheeks.

"How about this?" he said finally. "I won't help him. And then, when he comes after me, I'll kill him myself."

Valerie Fassero watched us like a movie, eating Chex mix.

"I just don't feel right calling," Sterling said uncomfortably.

"I don't feel right *not* calling," I replied.

The phone rang in his hand. We both flinched.

"Jesus *shit,* I hate that," he said, picking up. "Hello . . . Oh. Hi."

He looked at me and muttered, "Mother B." Then he said to the phone, "Well, no, as a matter of fact, I was just calling to rat him out."

"Don't put it on yourself," I hissed. "Tell her I'm the one."

He held a hand up.

"Look, ahh, Mom . . ."

"*Don't* call her that, don't encourage her!"

". . . We're having an argument here over who gets to make the call, what does that tell you? . . . Well, he knows where to find me . . . Okay, gotta run. Tell Lester he's gotta run too . . . Okay . . . Bye."

He hung up and said, "She's not mad—just disappointed. She says Lester'll be mad. It doesn't matter which of us calls now."

After he dialed the toll-free number and relayed our Lester Bogle sighting, he walked over to Valerie Fassero.

"You need to leave," he told her mildly. "I have this bad-tempered relative who doesn't care about guests, or bystanders, he just expresses himself in a, in a rotating spray."

"Then let's go out," she said.

Even when he clarified the situation, she still didn't back away. She'd been working in bar-code scanners for so long she was ready for anything.

I felt otherwise. As I drove to Abby's parents' house, and over the course of the next couple days, I did some pretty tense thinking.

Lester was the first killer I'd ever met, that I

knew of, and his remark about my family stayed with me. It made me think of all the true crime stories at the bookstore. There's so many of them. You don't think "That couldn't happen to me" anymore; instead you're surprised it hasn't happened to you already.

I was concerned about Maggie's exposure, and Abby's. To me it was a situation that clearly called for the full-body Spudge-Face Safety Suit.

CHAPTER TEN

Abby and Maggie stayed with the Zanes in Anaheim Hills for a week. I went from our place to work and back, and talked to them every day on the phone.

Abby took it all pretty well, considering. She had a right to be mad. She'd taken pains prior to marriage to make sure she wasn't getting linked to anyone moody, and now here came Lester, a remote connection, out of the bleachers. He was just the type she objected to.

Her last boyfriend before Ken Bender used to become violently enraged whenever she laughed at another man's jokes. For a while she thought it was her fault that she antagonized this boyfriend so much, but finally one day, as she sat in a broom closet he'd locked her in, she had what we in AA call a moment of clarity and resolved that if she ever got out of that closet, she'd run. After she got away from him, he trailed her briefly, but fortunately he was already in the process of transferring his attention to another woman.

Abby could have given me a hard time about Lester; I'd assured her that she wasn't marrying into the company of any such person. But she just nodded calmly when we discussed what to do, and the only time she became vehement was when I said I might get a gun. She refused to let Maggie return to a house with a gun in it. I didn't press the point. I didn't agree with her projections—I would *not* have shot the Sparkletts man—but I had to acknowledge the potential for an accident.

So for the week that I stayed home alone, and for quite a while after, I did what Sterling and I used to do when we lived with Dad; I carried a few stones in my jacket pockets. I am extremely accurate with rocks and stones, having thrown things fairly ceaselessly throughout my youth. I was a Little League pitcher and my control was excellent, side-arm or three-quarters. You never completely lose that.

The rocks didn't figure to provide much protection against Lester if he chose to open up on me from down the block, but it gave me some reassurance to feel them in my jacket. I could go to work.

Sterling wasn't as worried about Lester as I was. He didn't fear for his body. He once did a "high fall" stunt leap off a fifteenth-floor ledge, which I wouldn't do even if I wanted to kill myself. His only big fear was a specific kind of performance anxiety involving live television. Compared to that,

Lester Bogle was small spuds. So Sterling kept his address, his phone number and his usual irregular hours. He spent some time with Valerie Fassero, although he rarely let her come to his place.

He wasn't afraid of Lester; but he was, I would say, floored by recent events. He seemed stupefied. He couldn't stop thinking about being Vincent Charles Bogle.

I'm attaching a few pictures of Maggie to this manuscript so you'll be able to see the resemblance between her and me. There may be an even stronger resemblance between her and you.

At this time she was three and a half, with big hazel eyes. She was healthy, but small and lean, with these little bones—a central nervous system with a thin skin overlay. It was poignant that she envisioned herself as Kimberly, the Pink Power Ranger, kicking and jumping. She could just about fight her way out of a pullover pajama top.

Sometimes she reminded me of me. On her birthday it was like watching myself open presents. And sometimes she reminded me of you, or of the idea of you. I hadn't given much thought to you for years. It was only after she was born, and especially after I met the Bogles, that my curiosity truly returned. I could see that Sterling was all in knots, believing that as a Bogle he might not be in the tip-top genetic percentile. I wondered what I was passing on to Maggie.

Still, during these days I worried more about her environment than her heredity. I couldn't forget Lester's reference to my family.

I didn't think he could get Maggie into a car, say, by waving a Barbie doll or candy at her. She was suspicious of strangers, and she thought dolls looked weird. But if he said he had a kitten, or a chipmunk, she'd follow him anywhere. She'd crawl over broken glass to see a chipmunk. The thought kept me awake.

I don't mean to go on about the depth of my fatherly feeling. I'd been a dad long enough so that I didn't hear music every time I looked at Maggie. I got mad at her when she was bratty or demanding, and I couldn't play her games with her for more than twenty minutes without getting bored. But when I saw her looking at a storybook, or sitting on that little pony at the stable Abby took her to—Maggie always wore her brave expression then, while her heart bounced around her rib cage—I was stricken with love and fear. She had no shell. It hurt to have her and Lester Bogle in the same world.

I don't know if the Lesters have become a larger percentage of the population, but when you have more and more people, you naturally have more and more crazy people. And of course today they're much better armed.

So I concluded that my kid needed better armor.

Chadwick Mantle, in R&D, had been working with his staff on the full-body Spudge-Face Baby Safety Suit—a padded child's uniform using a flexible but impenetrable ceramic gel which was so light it actually floated in the air. The morning after meeting Lester I was down there hollering at Chad to hurry the hell up with the prototype.

And to make it cute. It had to be cute, so Maggie would wear it. We had already had trouble with her when it came to wearing our other products. Elston Petty had been appalled to hear that Maggie often played on the jungle gym at Oriole Park without her helmet and visor. He wanted the Little Spudge-Face girl to wear her Spudge-Face paraphernalia in public at all times.

At the time, Abby had taken Maggie's side, saying she didn't want her turning into a wimp like Elston's daughter, who wore all the Spudge-Face products and looked like Plan 9 from Outer Space.

"Bruyana Petty cries all the time," said Abby. "These products are not for constant wear."

After meeting Lester, though, I came down firmly on Elston's side in the controversy. After a few days I got the first Little Spudge-Face Baby Safety Suit from Chad Mantle, snuck it out of the office and took it over to Abby's parents' house.

Maggie didn't want to put it on. It was big and gray and to her it looked like a trap. I said it was just like a Power Ranger suit, but she was extremely knowledgeable about Power Ranger suits and straightened me out.

Abby and I finally jammed her into it, and she looked pretty safe. If her body were to get jolted or wrenched suddenly, or flung at a certain velocity— if, for instance, her horse ran away with her, and then stopped abruptly and she flew over its head— small transparent blister units within the lining would puff out automatically to cushion her, in a mini-airbag effect. If somebody stabbed her, the ceramic gelatin packing would prevent any puncture.

Her eyes were protected by the goggles, her head by the helmet, her hands by the gloves, her feet by the boots and her groin by the mesh trunks. All in all she was cute as a bunny.

"She can't get any oxygen to her body," Abby said critically. "Her skin is going to rot."

We watched her try to get the helmet off.

"Nobody knows we're here," said Abby. "Why can't she wear regular clothes here?"

Maggie did look uncomfortable, yanking up on her headpiece. I could hear her gritting out, "Daa-ad!" in rising anger and panic.

I walked over and turned the jaw tabs so they were horizontal. The headpiece flew back, revealing Maggie's face, in tears. She socked me in the thigh.

"It wouldn't come *off*!"

"You just have to turn the tabs, honey, like this. Then it easily flips back."

"I hate it, it's *hot*."

"It's so you'll be safe, honey. Wear it for Dad. Just for a day or two."

"It's scratchy!" She was starting to panic again, trying to climb out of it.

"For a Magic Mane Pony?"

Maggie liked these ponies that used to be $12.99 at the store but didn't get an animated TV show and so had come down to $3.99. She didn't care that they weren't on TV; she liked them for themselves.

Her face took on a cautiously hopeful expression under the tear tracks.

"Two?" she suggested.

"Well . . . one a day."

"One a *day*?" She was flabbergasted.

"Daa-ad," said Abby, gritting her teeth and pulling me a few steps away.

"Oh, like you never bribed her," I muttered back. "I want her in that suit until they catch Lester. And you too."

"Pardon?"

"Chad's preparing small, medium and large female adult. I'm getting you one."

"Oh, fine, we'll make a— Did you say large?"

I had to retract that—I hadn't meant anything by it—and the next day I had to take the prototype back and tell Chad to punch holes in it or soften the material or something. Maggie just wouldn't wear it, even for Magic Mane ponies.

I visited Sterling at the end of that week. I remember zigzagging up to his door in what I took to be evasive action, in case Lester was watching. I did something odder than that: I bent over and sniffed at the doorknob before I touched it.

Sterling was home, watching TV, but he might as well have been staring at the wall. He was inert.

I asked what was new, and he said his new mother phoned him daily. At first the calls had focused upon his refusal to help Lester, and characterized him as a traitor to the family. She said Lester had left the area, that it had been ruined for him. She hoped Sterling was satisfied, and warned that Denny had predicted a reckoning.

After that she had gradually mellowed and eventually took to confiding freely in Sterling. She told him all about her medical history and her neighbors, whom she detested.

Sterling relayed this to me without emotion or oomph. He seemed deflated. I asked him if he wanted to get out of the house and go to the beach with Abby, Maggie and me, but he said he was going to stay and watch an old "Columbo."

A day or so later I called Mom and told her what had been going on. There was a long pause on the other end.

"Well, if one mother isn't enough for him I'm sure he's welcome to her," she said finally.

"Mom, he's not *happy* about it. Her other son's a killer. Didn't you see Ster when he did the guy on 'Open Cases'?"

"No, I thought I'd wait until he did a comedy."

I asked Mom if the name "Bogle" rang a bell, and she said, irritably, that she didn't know, and then maybe, and then yeah, it sounded familiar. "Bogle or Gobel. It wasn't Gable." She said she no longer had the adoption documentation, that Dad had had it and lost it or buried it and that she couldn't remember her own name half the time.

"Well, I'm a little curious about myself too, Mom, because Maggie, you know, has that red, wrinkly thing on her hands that I do. And I was wondering if my birth parents had any condition that might affect her."

"Oh, my, yes. Didn't I just see a movie-of-the-week about someone who passed chapped hands on to his child?"

"All right. Skip it."

"No, I'll try and find out for you. God forbid you should live in the present."

Although I sympathized with Sterling, I didn't really understand his state of mind at that time. I wondered why he didn't just shake it off after a few days and go back to being himself. But his discovery had separated us more than I initially realized; he had gone beyond the idle speculation we both used to indulge in. He now knew his origin, and that made us different.

Recently I caught up a little; I learned my birth name. But my feeling still wasn't exactly comparable to Sterling's when he found out he was a Bogle. He was confronted not only with a new name, but with the people who went with it. I mean, there was Lester right in front of him, like a mirror at the fun house.

CHAPTER ELEVEN

Abby and Maggie moved back home after that week, and we got a security system which set off a high, loud, piercing tone and alerted the police if anyone opened the windows or doors while it was on. We were satisfied with it; it worked every time we accidentally set it off. I also augmented my throwing rocks with a softball bat. Dad had kept one for intruders when Sterling and I were little, but mine was aluminum.

As it turned out, the only one who tried to break in was a mild old gentleman from the nearby retirement community who had gone out for dinner and forgotten where he lived. He pounded on our front window at 2 A.M. I turned on the porch light, bat at the ready, but we ended up pals. And we closed out 1994 without hearing from Lester.

Sterling kept on doing stunts, or "gags," as he

called them, but gradually stopped auditioning for real parts; his only acting was as a ringmaster opposite Maggie's lion in a circus act in our apartment for Christmas.

At work, we initiated discussions on how best to introduce the recently improved, aerated, less itchy Little Spudge-Face Baby Safety Suit. Chad Mantle had acted on Maggie's criticisms and the thing was now practically comfortable.

Elston felt—all of us at Little Spudge-Face felt—that we should do something special in the way of an ad campaign. This was our masterpiece, our deluxe, top-of-the-line product. Nobody at the office mentioned it without using the phrase "cutting edge" or something about pushing an envelope. Our head of marketing, Claire Simon, said that we should make the new commercials more professional, without losing the warmth that was the core of Little Spudge-Face's appeal.

Claire proposed a TV spot in which a kid wearing the suit would fall out of a moving car or get pulled down the street at the end of a dog leash, and then get up unhurt.

I thought Elston was going to strike her right there in his office or I would've done it myself.

"You're not pushing my kid out of a car," I said.

"No, with *graphics*. *Jeez*," said Claire. "Come into the light."

Claire often revealed impatience with my thinking. A marketing veteran at twenty-eight, she thought I'd come into my job through the friend-of-the-boss entrance, which of course I had. She was blond, with a pointy face and a pretty figure. In her previous job, at an ad agency, she had engineered the campaign for Pensa-Cola, a drink that makes you more creative. Elston generally deferred to her thinking on promotional matters.

In this instance, though, he was in my corner: "We don't even *simulate* those things happening to a child."

"Well, how are you going to demonstrate the suit?" asked Claire.

Elston thought for a moment.

"Put a monkey in it," he said. He didn't have the same feeling for animals that he did for children.

"We'd get in more trouble doing that with a monkey than we would with a kid," said Claire.

"How about a human adult?" I suggested.

"Prisoners," said Elston, brightening.

"No, an actor," I said. "I mean, the suit is safe, right?"

"Of *course* it's safe," said Elston, indignantly.

"Okay," said Claire. "We have a guy put on the suit and do these things, and then he gets up and says something, so you can see he's all right. He says like, 'Gee, that was refreshing,' or—"

"Or something about the suit."

"Yeah. He goes, 'If your child was wearing this, you could drop him out of a second-story window.' "

"No. He says, 'If this suit protects me, it'll protect your baby. Because I'm just a big baby myself.' "

I said that, and Elston stared at me.

"Did you make that up?"

I shrugged modestly.

"What was it again?" he asked.

"If you're wearing this—no. If your baby is wearing this suit . . . you'll be fine . . . What the hell did I say?"

Claire said it was too long anyway.

"I wish we were doing better," said Elston moodily.

"We'll get it," said Claire confidently. "It'll come. Sometimes it takes hours, sometimes days. Then suddenly it's there, like 'Just do it.' "

As we searched for the proper way to introduce the Spudge-Face Baby Safety Suit to the world, early in 1995, Orange County went bankrupt and Doug McClure died.

The bankruptcy upset Elston, as did the voters' refusal to help pay it off with a half-cent increase in sales tax. There was a lot of talk in the papers about how with less money available for county law enforcement, young offenders and other criminals would be released from jail early, or not arrested at all.

"The time for the Little Spudge-Face Suit is *now*," he told me as February began. "And once we've got this product off the ground, we're moving this company out of here. I'm not raising my daughter in a county that refuses to wipe its own ass."

Unsettling as the bankruptcy was, I knew Sterling would be hit harder by the passing of Doug McClure, who had been a regular visitor to our boyhood living room for years as Trampas, the Shiloh ranch top hand, on "The Virginian." As an adult, Sterling had occasionally watched "Virginian" reruns on cable, commenting that the "Trampa-sodes" held up well.

I called Sterling on the afternoon of February 7, the day the obituary appeared; I hadn't seen him since Christmas and thought he might want company. He told me he was going to the Anaheim Public Library and to meet him there. I found him gimping along the reference shelves, walking with a bandaged ankle.

"Sorry about Doug McClure," I said.

"Who cares about Doug McClure?"

I was taken aback.

"You do," I said.

He lurched past me, carrying a thick Encyclopedia Britannica volume, the one labeled "Chicago to Death." I followed him to a table, where he sat and leafed through it until he reached "Criminality—causes, biological and hereditary." As he leafed, he spoke with quiet bitterness.

"It's indicative of the futility of my life that you should say, 'Sorry about Doug McClure.' Did we *know* Doug McClure? Was he in any way, to us, a real person? No—except that he was one of the gallery of Trivial Pursuit answers I've wasted half my life thinking about. I mean, who *cares* how good the Trampa-sodes were?"

"I hear you," I said quietly, to set an example.

"You know," he went on, "I used to hate it when people like Lee Ann said 'Who cares' or 'So what' about my enthusiasms, but they were just trying to tell me something. 'Who cares' means: nobody cares. It's a waste of time. We have to concentrate on real people. How are Abby and

Maggie. Things like that. So when you say to me, 'Sorry about Doug McClure,' what you're *really* saying is 'Sorry your life is so barren that you have to dwell on forgotten stars of mediocre television shows of the sixties.' "

"I don't know. I thought he was pretty good."

"Well, he was. He was underrated, goddamn it."

A passing librarian asked us to tone it down a notch, and Sterling sat motionless for a moment, looking attentive.

"What are you doing?" I asked.

"I had a little flash there, a little urge," he said.

"Urge to what?"

"When she said, 'Could you please quiet down.' A little—" He raised his fist and jabbed it forward a couple inches. "That's my heritage. Felt the same way in the 'Manhattan Live' locker room. Just like Lester. I wanted to—" He unobtrusively mimed machine-gunning the room.

"Oh, for Christ's sake."

He opened his palm to stop me, found a relevant section and followed it with his index finger.

" 'The suggestion of genetic influences in criminal behavior,' " he read, " 'is supported by studies of adopted children.' "

"You're telling the room," I said.

" 'The rate of criminality was higher among those adopted children who had one biological parent who was criminal than among those who had one adoptive parent who was criminal.' " He sat back.

"So?" I said.

"So there it is. The wiring carries the weight. Joe Bogle, the line-blower, and Loretta, whom you met, begat Lester and me, and to my mind, much is explained thereby." He thumped the book shut.

I was exasperated.

"Come *on*. You go back a ways, there's a criminal in every family. And probably a line-blower too."

"Yeah, but I got the immediate breeding."

"That's dumb."

He sniffed at me.

"Easy for you to say. You still think you're the Crown Prince of Potsdorf."

He got up and gimped the book back to its place on the shelf. As we left the building, I asked about his leg.

"Ahhh, I got blown up last week and I didn't land right." We went a few more steps and he added, "Fact is, they kicked me off the picture. Co-ordinator said I'm not careful enough. These are stunt people and all they talk about is careful."

He told me Mother Bogle had taken to visiting at unpredictable intervals. Denny would drive her over. Sterling wouldn't let Denny in, but he couldn't bring himself to turn Loretta away. So he'd cook her a meal, and later Denny would come back and drive her home to San Juan Capistrano.

He checked his watch. "She's there now. I told her I was going out but she said she'd wait. We're having Stouffer's biscuits with gravy."

"What do you talk about?"

"Oh, mostly how hard it is to raise kids."

"Where's Lester?"

"We don't know. But we miss him."

He said he had something at home to show me, so I followed him back to his place. Ma Bogle was there, watching TV, comfy on the couch. She greeted me pleasantly.

"Are you on tonight, Vinnie?" she asked Sterling.

"No," he said, and went into the kitchen.

"Sometimes we see him flying through the air or running up a hill," she told me. "I make him point himself out. You stick with that stunt work, honey," she called to him. "That's the difference between having a nickel and asking for one."

I hung around while Sterling made her a biscuit with gravy, but it was depressing to hear her call him Vinnie. He seemed resigned to the name when she was around. Sterling Fleger became indistinct. He even seemed lumpy, as if he were putting on weight from cooking and sharing the food Mrs. Bogle preferred. I didn't care for the alteration. "Vinnie" had a wholly different sound, to me, than Sterling. Vinnie Bogle sounded like a guy who hangs out on the corner until he's told to move on.

In the kitchen he showed me a note he'd received from Lester, in an envelope postmarked San Francisco. The individual letters in the message had been cut out of a magazine and glued to the page, which seemed unnecessary since it was obvious who it was from. It took a minute to decipher, though, because some of the letters had come unglued and fallen into the crease. This gave the note a kind of "Wheel of Fortune" quality; Sterling was addressed as a "moth fucker." It began, "I'm not here"—

meaning San Francisco, I guess—and ended up "ne time som ody el e will ha to p ay my part."

"Have you shown it to the cops?"

"Yeah, they thought it was pretty funny. One of them said, 'I'd like to solve the puzzle.' "

"What about *catching* him?"

"I hope they don't. I hope he comes back. I hope he comes right through that door."

He leaned back against the sink and gazed at the kitchen door, his arms folded.

"I did some research on the guy he killed. Guy ran a French restaurant. That's a lot of headaches, you know—a restaurant. I drove down to San Clemente, I went past it. And I parked. But I was ashamed to go in."

"Lester's not your responsibility. You never even knew him."

"I know him now, the little moth fucker."

I thought Sterling needed a role to play other than Vinnie Bogle, so when Elston, Claire Simon and I next met at the office to discuss a spokesperson and demonstrator for the Spudge-Face Safety Suit, I decided to recommend him.

Elston wanted Tom Hanks or Bill Cosby. Claire, reading from what she called her "real world" list, suggested Chevy Chase.

"How about Sterling Ahummerum?" I asked.

Halfway through "Sterling" I realized my recommendation might be downgraded if I gave his real name, so I closed with a throat-clearing cough. I didn't know if Elston would use another Fleger after me, Maggie and Abby.

"Who?" asked Claire.

"Guy's name is Sterling . . . I've seen him, he's really good. He was in 'Slugs,' and he's been on 'Open Cases.' And he can do his own stunts."

"Thought you wanted a star," said Claire to Elston.

"I do," said Elston.

"No star," I declared, "is going to fall off a building or rappel down a mountain in the Little Spudge-Face Suit."

"Doesn't anyone have any confidence in the *product*?" asked Elston indignantly.

We discussed several possibles but couldn't reach a decision. I was the only one who advocated Sterling Ahummerum. Elston finally adjourned us, sending Claire off to find the right big name to embody the Spudge-Face idea.

The next week she announced her search concluded, and invited Elston and me to join her for dinner at Chasen's in Beverly Hills, where she said we were to meet "the guy"; she wouldn't tell us who it was. It was to be a surprise. When Elston asked, "Is it somebody big?" Claire said, "Hey, he got us a table."

This was an impressive achievement. It was four days before the '95 Oscars, and Chasen's was the most difficult reservation in Greater Hollywood because the famous old restaurant was about to close down and all the movie industry insiders were jamming into it one last time. It was said to be impossible to get in for dinner, but our mystery spokesman had reserved us a booth for four.

I drove Elston up there from work that Thursday night; Claire had said she'd meet us. I was eager to see the restaurant, and to see what Hollywood luminary she had found for us. So when we got to Chasen's and went in, I hurried on ahead into the first dining area while Elston checked his coat, and immediately found myself confronting Steven Spielberg, sitting by himself in a booth facing the door, regarding me with a kind of amiable, wistful expression.

I was surprised that a person as popular and successful as Steven Spielberg should be sitting there all alone, and astounded that he wanted to wear our Little Spudge-Face suit in a commercial. I was incredibly impressed with Claire. This was far beyond what I'd expected; I'd thought she'd lined up maybe Lou Ferrigno. I was about to stretch my hand over the table and welcome Steven aboard when several other people, including, I believe, his partners in the DreamWorks studio, appeared beside me and slid into the booth with him, and I saw he wasn't stuck for company after all. I recovered with a smooth pivot as Elston caught up with me, and we went on past, toward the bar in the back.

Chasen's was packed, each booth filled and two and three deep at the bar, but it had a mellow atmosphere to it. The booths were cushy and the walls had pictures of the greats who had eaten there, like Liz Taylor, and Lew Wasserman when he was young. I didn't see anyone leaping around collecting autographs, however. The impression I got was that a celebrity could sit there and eat his dinner. You could gawk from your table but you weren't to harass him unless you knew him.

Claire was seated about halfway to the bar, her hair and eyes shining. She waved Elston and me into the booth and I sat down across from our new Spudge-Face star, Art Klee.

He was heavier and tanner than he had been the last time I'd seen him in person, in the "Manhattan Live" locker room twenty years before. He had since made several movies—a couple successful ones and then a few more which had gently declined in quality and profitability. He was still a star, though, and Claire was clearly tickled to be there at Chasen's with him. Elston too was impressed, and relieved to recognize him.

My feeling was more complex.

Klee didn't recognize me, of course. In fact he hardly saw me; he was scanning the room like everyone else. He shook my hand when we were introduced and said, "Isn't this something? We got people here came out of the grave."

There were indeed several attendees who might have dined there with Bogart in days gone by. People from old and new Hollywood stared at one another. Later, when I went to the men's room, they eyed me too. They weren't disappointed at not recognizing me, either; more intrigued, assuming I must amount to something or I couldn't have gotten in.

Klee told movieland gossip through drinks and the iced seafood plate. Our heads whipped around every time someone walked by. Once it was Peter Graves, and after that I was even more vigilant.

It struck me that this was the kind of deal-meal Sterling had pictured when he was a kid, when he

said we'd have lunch someday with Steve McQueen.
I thought Sterling should have been there instead of
me. I thought he should have been there instead of
Klee.

"Don't like the shellfish?" Klee asked me finally, when I didn't join the laughter at his descrip-
tion of one director as the stupidest man who ever
made more than $12,000 a year.

"No," I said. "I'm just thinking about the other
time we met."

"Did we?"

"Yeah, I tried to sock you."

He leaned forward to get a better look at me,
then shrugged.

"At a party? I had a few years there where I
saw everybody, like, through cellophane. Sorry I
don't—"

"After the Charles Manson bit in New York,"
I said.

"The Charles—" Klee's eyes slowly widened.
"Whoa. Are you that guy who choked?"

"I'm his brother."

"Wow," he said softly, transported back in
time.

"You know each other?" asked Claire. It was
the first time she'd ever looked impressed with me.

"I'll never forget it," said Klee. "Worst moment
I ever had onstage. Whatever happened to that guy?
I thought maybe he'd go live in the South Seas."

"He went into another career for a while. Now
he's an actor again."

"Tell him to stick with film," Klee said pleasantly. "You get to do it over."

"Tell him yourself and see what he does," I said, irritated.

Claire goggled at me, but Klee wasn't offended. He even laughed.

"He'd probably deck me again," he said.

"What you said to him was worth a beating," I replied.

Claire gave me a soccer-style kick under the table. Klee's eyes half-closed.

"Well, your brother coughed it up, you know," he said blandly. "Some guys are great Ping-Pong players, but if you tell 'em the loser buys the beer, then they can't play." He shook his head reminiscently. "Tell ya, I was pissed. That bit has stayed with me. I was supposed to be able to handle anything onstage, that was a point of pride. But when he said 'Manson,' he set me on my ass." To the others, he added, "After the show he did it again."

"I woulda killed you after what you said," I told him.

Klee's brow furrowed.

"I'm trying to remember what I did say. Something critical? You'da killed me, huh?"

"Oh, I don't know," I said. "It's an expression."

"Art, I know Elston here is excited about you as the Spudge-Face Baby," said Claire, moving away from my reminiscent vein of conversation.

"This is a comedy spot, right?" asked Klee.

"Your character gets into high-impact situations," explained Claire, "and emerges unhurt, so parents can see that their children would be safe in the suit."

Klee nodded judiciously. We all stared as Bob Hope moved slowly, but with determination, through the tables on the other side of the room. Now I *really* wished Sterling was there. Sterling always agreed with Woody Allen's assessment of Hope's early work.

"How do we do it? Graphics or a double?" asked Klee.

"Well . . . ," said Claire, glancing at Elston, "we do it for real, so the viewer can see that the suit works."

Klee laughed. Then he laughed some more.

"So. Twenty years later," he said to me, "your elaborate revenge. I put on this suit and you Super-Dave me."

Elston overrode my denial.

"I don't know what you mean," he said. "Our engineers have crafted the single most injury-resistant piece of human attire in history."

"Well done," said Klee. "But I don't stunt. I mean, I'd love to step on the third rail for you, but they won't let me."

"Do you have children, Mr. Klee?" asked Elston.

"Yeah," he admitted.

"You can't do anything more important than provide for the safety of your children. For *everyone's* children."

Klee shrugged.

"I'll say the lines, and do the reactions, you know. But my double takes the falls. That's just the way it is."

"Elston," said Claire, "I don't see a downside

here. If his double takes the impact and gets up, clearly unhurt, to face the camera, then our story is told, and we can cut to a close-up of Art saying the lines with that great spin of his. It'll have super resonance."

Elston considered it.

"All right," he said finally. "But let me clarify something for Mr. Klee."

"Art."

"Art, we are selling a product, yes. But we are not *foisting*. We address a need. We are not pushing a new kind of . . . *chip*."

"Okay," said Klee, nodding. "The only thing *I* have to clarify is that I will not get into any crate that *he*"—pointing to me—"puts the wing nuts on. He wants to get me. Don't ya?"

I shook my head. I really didn't. It was all so long ago.

As we walked out, Klee leaned toward me and muttered, "Tom Hanks." It was too—at a corner table with Martin Short and a bunch of other people. *Forrest Gump* won all those Oscars the following Monday night. I couldn't see Hanks's face, but I recognized the side of the back of his head.

Shortly afterward, Elston officially okayed Art Klee as the Spudge-Face spokesperson. I called Sterling and told him about it, in hopes that the mention of Klee's name might get his hackles up and start his blood circulating again.

"Well, the guy's a talent," he said, and then was silent.

"We'll be doing stunts," I said. "Interested?"

"Ahh, I don't know. I've got enough money for a few months, and my ankle's still sore. Think I'll take it easy for a while."

"Okay. Just thought I'd ask."

"Okay. Say hi to Abby and Maggie."

"Okay."

"Okay."

Okay then, I thought. Okay, Vinnie.

CHAPTER TWELVE

After ten months of testing we introduced the Little Spudge-Face Baby Safety Suit in early '96, in a national commercial featuring Art Klee and his double, a guy named Nat Castleman. We showed Klee in the suit, as an overgrown child walking with his mother atop one of the Hollywood Hills. Then he began a pratfall and we showed Nat Castleman in *his* suit, rolling and caroming all the way down the hill to the bottom. We cut back to the "mother" reacting every time he hit an obstruction.

Nat finally fetched up at the foot of the hill, and slowly stood. We cut to the gratified old lady playing his mother, standing at the summit and looking down. Then we cut back to Art Klee, standing where Nat had been, screaming upward at the very top of his lungs:

"Didn't hurt!"

Then he turned to the camera and said, "How's *your* little spudge-face?"

In other commercials, we had Nat doing things that kids might do, like tumbling off a jungle gym, falling face first onto a big sharp-cornered table and chasing a ball into the street and running into a parked truck. Each time, Nat would get to his feet, then we'd cut to his mother (or father) and back to Klee saying his lines.

The lines rarely varied. It was a very simple, repetitive campaign. Everybody got to know it. It gave Art Klee more exposure than he'd had in years, and presented him as a nice guy.

Abby and Maggie took their replacement as Spudge-Face singer and Spudge-Face girl gracefully. Maggie had been on TV since she could remember; she was glad it was over because it bored her. And Abby, although she didn't say so, had never really cared for the Spudge-Face song. She felt about singing it pretty much the way Pernell Roberts used to feel about doing "Bonanza." She had made a little money and we had banked some for Maggie's college, so, she said, we had nothing of which to complain. I could see she was looking forward to singing some real music instead of my croup jingles.

At the office, everyone was thrilled. Sales were strong from the get-go, and other shows and comedians added to our name recognition when they parodied the Art Klee commercials. Claire became ecstatic when Leno and Letterman started making fun of us.

There was some criticism of the Safety-Suit concept as paranoid, neurotic and inhibiting to children's freedom to play unencumbered, but Elston had been prepared for that. "Tell it to a mother whose kid just fell out of a tree," he said.

And there was some carping about the base price—$1,995. Elston's response: "It's a rock-bottom margin for us. That's a public-service price. I defy any other company to bring in a suit of that quality for less."

Other companies tried. The first knockoffs were the Cutie-Pie Suit and another one called the Muffin Cover—but they either skimped on material, padding or accessories. We were the Beatles; they were the Monkees.

Elston said that it looked like year-end bonuses for sure. Abby and I went and looked at a house; for the first time we thought of buying instead of renting.

And then, in July, a consumer magazine called *Buyer Beware* challenged us. Their staff did its own experiments and concluded that the safety suit wasn't foolproof.

Elston was furious.

"Of *course* it isn't foolproof!" he exploded the day the magazine came out. "If your child is determined to destroy himself, he can do it even in the suit. If he crawls out onto the freeway and lets car after car run over him . . . If he goes to sleep in the refrigerator, eventually the auxiliary oxygen is going to be exhausted."

"They think we're faking the stunts somehow," I said, reading it.

"This is what comes of helping people," said Elston, nodding to himself as he stared at his office poster of Great Moments in Medicine. "This is the thanks all innovators get. Vilification. Ridicule. Crucifixion."

I felt bad for him. Nobody had the Spudge-Face spirit like Elston Petty. He personally oversaw every department—R&D, production, promotion and distribution. He was vigilant. He took a hands-on approach. Everybody at the office dreaded his approach. It was unjust for this report to imply that he was cynical or cutting corners. Elston put everything into the company.

He and his wife Joanne and little Bruyana lived on the Balboa peninsula in Newport Beach, facing the harbor. Joanne Petty had long, straight blond hair and a contemplative kind of expression. The first time I met her, at a Christmas party, she stared at me for a while and finally said, "I'll bet you're an old soul." Their home was childproof except for the living room, which had sculpture and glass-topped tables. Bruyana wasn't allowed in there. On our first visit, Abby and Joanne stayed in the living room while Elston showed me around, and by the time we got back, the wives were old pals.

"She says she's only had three orgasms with him," Abby told me as we went home that night.

"Oh, jeez." I winced. I couldn't believe someone would confide that to a relative stranger. Joanne Petty had had fewer conversations with Abby than she'd had orgasms with Elston.

"There wasn't much preamble," Abby admitted. "I said something about how dedicated he seemed to be, and pow. Out it came."

"Well, I hope you told her we've lost count."

"I just listened to her. She says he used to try harder, and now it's like he's given up."

"Does she want us to *do* something about this, or was she just shooting the breeze?"

"I think she just needed someone to talk to. Elston is so totally obsessed with Spudge-Face."

And he was. Not so much with the *success* of the company as with the *idea* of the company. Elston saw himself as co-father to the world. And when this magazine impugned his motives and methods, he was more than just mad; he was hurt. He would stand at his office window, looking down at the Pacific Coast Highway, for most of a morning.

It was at this time, while he was incensed and wounded, that the idea came to him to perform a demonstration so vivid and spectacular that no one could dismiss it.

He called Claire Simon and me into his office one morning some time after the *Buyer Beware* report came out, and told us he'd decided to shoot Art Klee out of a cannon down the Las Vegas Strip on New Year's Eve.

"We'll televise it. Let's see 'em sneer at that," he said, standing tall at his desk. "When a man comes out of the sky in the Spudge-Face Suit and lands on the pavement, whap!, and then gets up and speaks to the camera . . . let's see 'em denigrate *that*."

As he described the stunt, Elston illustrated it by waving his arm in a huge arc and slamming his palm down flat, with a loud slap, on his desktop. Then, on the "gets up and speaks to the camera" part, he raised his wrist and finger-walked toward his other hand, which was poised on the desk with three fingers down to indicate a camera on a tripod.

For the first time in my short career at Little Spudge-Face, I thought, Uh-oh. I expected Claire Simon to tactfully steer Elston back to rational discourse, but she just sat there looking thoughtful. She didn't even seem surprised.

He told us the inspiration had struck him that morning in the shower, when the soap shot out of his hand. He wanted to buy commercial airtime and do it live in Vegas, at midnight, as the New Year turned, in about four months.

I thought it was screwy. The suit had never been tested that way, and the stunt didn't have anything to do with life as we presently live it anyway.

"Kids don't get shot out of cannons," I said.

"All the more reason," said Elston. "If the suit works under those conditions, it'll work under lesser ones."

"Did you say land on the pavement?" I asked.

"I did," said Elston. "The blister units will cushion the impact."

"Not enough," I said.

"You're forgetting the deluxe model with the manual double-puff option," said Elston, his voice rising. "And you're forgetting the quality of the Little Spudge-Face Baby Safety—"

"Klee won't do it," I said.

Elston seethed quietly.

"That timorous bastard," he said. "All right, the stuntman, then."

"Well, Elston, he can't say the lines," said

Claire, who had been silent up to now. "Believe me. I've talked to him. If you want him to hit the pavement and then give a professional reading, you're asking for trouble."

Elston came out from behind his desk and strode to the window.

"Enough of this counterproductive thinking," he stated grimly. "*I'll* do it. Put me in the suit, and shoot me from the Pelican to the Majestic Towers."

"Your heart," said Claire gently.

I hadn't known Elston had anything wrong with his heart, but on this issue Claire seemed to know him better than I did. He looked at her for a moment, and then looked out his window. There was a silence.

"You can't tell me," he said finally, turning back to us, "that there's no one who can do this."

"How about that guy, Sterling Ahummerum?" said Claire, turning to me. "Actor slash stuntman, right?"

"No," I said.

"What do you mean, no?" demanded Elston.

"Well, for one thing I wasn't completely candid about him. His name's Fleger, he's my brother, and he's the guy Art Klee was talking about at Chasen's. And I wouldn't feel right recommending him to get shot out of a cannon onto a city street."

This was too much for Elston, who now went sailing all over the office.

"In the *suit*!" he exploded. "For God's sake, I thought you of all people believed in the suit! I mean, if my inner circle—or has it always been this way, and I was just oblivious? Have I been surrounded from the beginning by people who don't trust the suit? Can that be?" He stared at me as if tentacles were popping out of my neck.

"I like the suit," I said evenly. "I don't like the stunt."

"If the stunt," said Claire, leaning forward in her chair to address me, "were made fail-safe, could your brother do it and say the line at the end?"

"It can't be made fail-safe," I said.

Elston now became the first person I've ever seen since Dad to actually tremble with rage.

"Get out," he told me. He pointed to the door, to guide me.

I blinked at him, uncertain.

"Beg pardon?" I asked.

"You are . . . to get away from me."

My face got hot. I stood up.

"Okay," I said, with dignity.

Then I went home.

That night Claire called me and said everything would be fine eventually, but for now it might be best if I got a little forty-eight-hour thing.

I stayed in bed the next morning. Abby put Maggie on the school bus, went to see her agent about a possible recording deal, came back to meet Maggie's bus, took her to the dentist, made dinner, watched her do her addition, read Berenstain Bears with her, tucked her in and got back in bed with me. Then she asked me why I was devoting so much attention to the ads for the new fall season. When I told her about my disagreement with Elston, I expected her to take my side, but she didn't.

"You shouldn't've just rejected his whole idea like that."

"Oh, right. I should tell 'em, 'My brother is the guy. You can shoot him anywhere.' "

"No, but what if it worked? Wouldn't that be good for Sterling? I mean, what's he doing?"

"Not much, but he's alive, so he can change his routine when he wants to."

We were quiet for a minute. I was uncomfortable, thinking maybe I'd done the wrong thing.

Sterling *hadn't* been doing much for the last year and a half. He did a stunt job now and then, but mostly he watched TV, either with Mrs. Bogle or Val Fassero or on his own. And even his TV watching had become lethargic. In the old days he'd been an *active* viewer, commenting freely on plot and portrayal, sometimes offering variations on a line reading. Back then, when he saw a wooden performance from Robert Stack, say, or a superficial one from Tony Franciosa, he'd cite earlier work they'd done in *Written on the Wind* or *Career* and chide their images for falling below their standard. Lately he just let it go. On his couch, where he spent most of his time, he looked similar to those older people you see sitting on benches and porches and in backyard chairs after a big meal on Sunday.

But he *was* still alive, and the stunt *was* stupid, and I told Abby that I wasn't going to recommend him for it, finis.

At which point the doorbell rang, and I finally got up. Unexpected nighttime visitors are my responsibility.

I didn't take my bat, because we'd stopped

watching for Lester. But I might have been able to use it at that, because my brother was on the welcome mat, swaying slightly, with his hands on his hips.

"Why don't I just kill ya?" he wanted to know.

We have a small room off the kitchen which Abby and Maggie and I use as a den for reading or resting or calming down if one of us is mad. After calling to Abby that it was only Sterling, I led him in there. He stood in the center of the room and glowered down at me.

"Did you or did you not—" he began in lawyerly fashion.

"Don't take that tone. And don't talk about killing me unless you're gonna try. I took it from Dad but I won't take it from you."

He switched to a sinister geniality while he scanned the books on the shelves.

"My agent got a call from Claire Somebody at your office, about a job. And he phoned me about it, and I said, 'Custodial?' And he said, 'No, stunting *and* acting, on *live* TV, in place of Art Klee. This Claire Somebody says your brother turned it down for you, but she wanted to discuss it anyway.' And I said"—Sterling cocked his head and took on a goofy, bucktoothed, puzzled look—" 'Turned it down for me? How *weird*.' "

"Are you loaded?" I asked him.

"I am pissed off," he said, waving the suggestion aside. "Everything else is extraneous."

"The job was to do a suicidal stunt for a commercial and say a couple lines at the end, if you survived. I didn't think it was doable, and I didn't think you'd be interested."

"You didn't."

"No, because you're a Bogle now and you just sit on your thumb."

He sniffed, moodily, and said nothing.

"You've got some stones," I went on, "coming over here like the fire chief after a year and a half of sitting on your ass. We've all tried to get you going. All you do is moan about your DNA."

"Well, I've decided I have to dismiss that," he said, quieter now. "I had a revelation. Why didn't you have them get in touch with me?"

"I didn't want to be responsible for your death."

"I can do a gag."

"Not this one," I said.

"How do you know?"

"I don't, but I suspect. It's a high fall with no cables—"

"Why didn't you let them talk to me?"

"I just said."

"Replacing Art Klee? With *lines*? *Live*? You know that's practically a takeover. Why didn't you let them talk to me?"

"I *told* you."

"Well, that's not good enough!"

"Okay, then, I thought you were wrong for the part, all right?"

He stared at me. I stared back. I hadn't consciously had that thought until I actually said it. Now I had to look it over. I sat down at the desk and gazed blankly at my gas bill.

I think somehow, subconsciously, all his talk about being wired to fail had seeped into my head, because when Claire had asked me at work if he could do the part, underneath my indignation at the risk involved I'd thought, Maybe not.

Anyway, that's what I saw on the gas bill.

Sterling goggled at me in disbelief.

"You didn't think I'd die doing the stunt," he said. "You thought I'd die doing the lines."

"Well, no, I thought the first was more likely."

He looked off to an invisible camera.

"My brother," he said.

All of a sudden everyone was recoiling from me, in horror at my disloyalty. And I guess they were right; I had shown a deficiency of faith in both the suit *and* my brother. But in Sterling's case, at least, it was because he had done the same. I still didn't understand his transformation from someone who wouldn't have cared to someone who did.

After he'd done a minute or two on the subject of my treachery, I went to the kitchen and made some coffee. He followed me. I asked what had caused the revelation he had mentioned, and he told me it was the way in which Valerie Fassero left him.

When they'd met, Valerie had thought of Sterling as a dynamic repository of feeling. But after he became a Bogle, his artistic initiative had disappeared. At first she'd made excuses for him while he sat and watched TV. She thought maybe he was studying different techniques. But as time went by she became disillusioned, and there'd been a final, disastrous rupture between them just days before, when he told her he might take a telemarketing job.

Valerie Fassero considered telemarketing the lowest form of acting.

"She said if she'd wanted some white-collar boiler-room geek, she'd have stayed with her husband," he said. "So she left. But first she came over to say good-bye. And to give me a going-away video. Know what it was?"

I thought for a moment.

"*Out of Africa?*"

He gave me Bewilderment.

"Why would it be *Out of Africa?*"

"I don't know. Romantic? Abby likes it."

"I didn't really expect you to guess. You won't guess it. I was going to tell you."

"Okay."

"*Prince of Players,* with Richard Burton. From the fifties."

I looked at him blankly, and he became impatient.

"Don't you get it?" he asked.

"Get what?"

"He played Edwin Booth."

"Uh-huh . . ."

Sterling waited, but I didn't leap in with anything further.

"Edwin Booth," he said distinctly. "The tragedian. His brother killed Lincoln, but he went on acting anyway. He didn't go into telemarketing."

"*Oh.*"

"She walked in, put the tape in the slot, said good-bye, and walked out the door."

"And what, you just sat there and watched it?"

"Well . . ." He looked at one of Maggie's

drawings on the refrigerator. "I thought she was better off. So yeah."

He opened the refrigerator, stared inside and closed it while he continued his story.

"Anyway," he said, "I'm neutral on Burton. I don't dislike him. I think he leaned on his voice, but that's beside the point. As I was watching, I got this moment." His eyes glazed over with a shocked realization, replaying the moment. "And I saw that if he could face an audience after his own brother, John Derek, shot Lincoln . . . well, I had no right to quit."

The thought once again struck me that Valerie Fassero spoke to Sterling in a way no other woman had.

"I called her up to thank her," he continued bleakly, "but I guess she's really left me. She said she never goes back. 'I never go back.' Then I heard about this job. And I thought, if I did that, maybe she'd, y'know, break precedent. And *then* they said you'd turned it down for me."

"Well, shit, *I* don't know," I said, uncomfortably. "The goddamn fool wants to shoot somebody out of a cannon and land him a block and a half up the street on the concrete."

"He must think it can work."

"Well, yeah, *he* does."

Sterling nodded, and looked around the room. There was a little pause.

"This is a nice place," he said.

"You've been here."

"Yeah, but it's starting to hit me. Pictures on the fridge . . ."

"The new Fleger dynasty," I said and nodded.

"It's like you righted yourself, somewhere. I mean, before, you always seemed like . . ."

"A double blank? A called third strike?"

"You turned it around."

"Hard to spot exactly where. All my big moments are little, I guess."

He took a deep breath. He seemed momentarily defenseless.

"Anyway, about this job . . . I guess I'm asking," he said. Then he winced, disgusted with himself.

Well, if your big brother as much as got down on his knees . . . I mean, he never asked me for *any*thing before.

I said I'd bring him in to interview with Claire and Elston. His eyes welled up a bit, I think largely because he'd had some beers previously.

"But I'm telling you," I warned him, "you probably won't live to say your lines."

"If I can't do one simple gag," he declared, "I'm a wussy, wimpy wienie."

"Okay."

"A prissy, pasty pansy-pussy."

"Gimme your keys."

I showed him to the living room couch, and he gave his attention to the living room TV, which was dark.

"Burton didn't live long enough to completely purify his work like Henry Fonda and James Garner did," he said. "You have to boil away everything stagy and work up through your heart."

I thought, He's seen so much TV he can watch it when it's off.

"You want AMC?" I asked. "You can have it on low."

"Nah, that's spoiled right now. Val and I used to watch it."

CHAPTER THIRTEEN

Sterling accompanied me into Elston's office the next day, clear-eyed and stalwart. He told Elston and Claire Simon that the children he hoped to have someday would be enveloped in the Spudge-Face line from day one, from Spudge-Face Swaddlers to the Spudge-Face Prom Night Defensive Driver-Pak.

"We don't have a Driver-Pak," said Claire.

"Well, the sooner you come up with one, the fewer seniors we'll lose," said Sterling.

Claire looked him over coolly.

"Art Klee says, 'How's your little Spudge-Face?' in a very distinctive way," she said. "Can you approximate it?"

"He's a great talent," said Sterling without emotion. Then he rose from his chair and became Klee, planting himself bulkily on the balls of his feet and thrusting his face forward aggressively.

"How's *your* little Spudge-Face?" he said, with a slight rasp, to Claire, who raised her eyebrows.

"That's very good." She looked at Elston, who nodded.

"Is that the only line?" asked Sterling.

"We haven't signed off on that yet," said Claire. "We might use 'Didn't hurt,' and we might not."

"Would I be doing Klee exactly, or would I have latitude to contribute a nuance or two?"

"For instance?"

"Oh, a wider smile at the end. A wave. A little extra brio."

"We can discuss it," said Claire.

Elston cleared his throat. He had one of Art Klee's Spudge-Face Suits there in his office, standing like Robocop in the corner.

"How does the idea of being shot out of a cannon in the LSBSS strike you?" Elston asked, looking keenly from the suit to me to Sterling. "Your brother feels it's too dangerous."

"Can I try it on?" asked Sterling.

We helped him into it, there in the office. I snapped the facial shield down myself. He walked away from us, over near Elston's Great Moments in Medicine poster. He twiddled his gloved fingers experimentally, and unsnapped the shield, raising it.

"This covers my face," he observed.

"Of course," said Elston.

"I open it after I land, don't I?"

Claire nodded.

"So the viewers can see you're not in pain. Of

course, if you *are* in pain, we'll want you to keep it on."

"The question," said Elston, "is whether you have faith in the product."

Sterling pointed across the room.

"Does that window open?"

We looked.

"No," said Elston.

Sterling walked to it and looked down.

"People down there," he said. "Never mind."

He snapped his facial shield shut and walked out of the office. We followed him past Reception, out the main door, into the hallway and through the exit door.

Elston, Claire and I stood in the stairwell and watched as Sterling somersaulted and caromed down the fire stairs, turning and tumbling at the foot of each flight, until he finally hit bottom, five floors down. Then he opened the shield and turned his face up toward us.

"Is there liquid in this?" he called. "It's got a kind of waterbed quality to it."

"That's the ceramic gel," Elston called down.

"You want me to go off the roof?"

"That won't be necessary," Elston responded, and smiled as he straightened up.

"I like that guy," he said.

Elston and Las Vegas were a good match. The town had recently been promoting itself as a more child-friendly place, with theme hotels and virtual reality rides; hosting the demonstration of a baby safety suit would point up this new slant. And the demonstration itself was totally in keeping with the kind of entertainment Las Vegas had come to stand for. Sort of circus-y, you know. Elston got starry-eyed picturing it. I think the Vegas people would have preferred to shoot Sterling through the air hand-in-hand with a showgirl, but the way Elston proposed it was good enough for them. When he pitched his idea, he got handshakes all around and a permit from the city to rope off the two blocks in front of the Majestic Towers on New Year's Eve.

Chad Mantle and his staff went out in the desert in Riverside County and began shooting Spudge-Face dummies into the sky, in preparation for Sterling's test flight.

Sterling himself didn't give much thought to the aspect of the event most people would dwell on—the landing. He only thought about his lines. After he was hired, he came to my office almost every day to chew on them.

" 'How's your little Spudge-Face?' Doesn't that sound tired to you?"

"It has the name of the company in it," I reminded him.

"But you'd have more impact with a new line."

"Like what?"

"Oh, like . . . 'Save your baby's bacon with—' No, 'Save your baby's *butt* with the Spudge-Face Safety Suit.' Baby's butt. Or something special for the circumstances. I'll have just landed from the sky. How about, 'As the Son of God . . .' "

Sterling was just feeling giddy that day, but it was odd that he should have said what he did, because I'd recently read in the paper that an

apocalyptic group called the Rapture Ascension-
ists—also known as the '96ers—expected Jesus
Christ to come down to earth right about the time
we'd be shooting Sterling down the Strip, at midnight New Year's Eve.

It seems this tiny but vocal sect or cult had determined through scriptural research that the righ-
teous spirits would ascend to heaven with the end
of the year 1996, that Jesus would be descending at
that time, and that shortly thereafter would come
the end of the world and the individual judging.

My own personal and imperfect understanding
of scripture is that the Bible says we aren't allowed
to know exactly when we'll all be reunited with the
Father. The '96ers had cracked that riddle, though.
They had even determined which midnight of all the
midnights in all the world's time zones on New
Year's Eve was the right one. They had chosen Desert Time. And they had chosen the sin town of Las
Vegas as the spot in which to greet the apocalypse
and rise above it.

I told Sterling that Jesus might be coming down
from the sky right about the time he was going up,
so he'd better watch his mouth.

"You're kidding," he said. My explanation
shut him up for about thirty seconds. He sat staring
at my office rug, pondering it.

"Well," he concluded finally, "I hope we go
first because I can't follow that."

Sterling's mothers, it developed, were unlikely
to attend the big event. When I called Mom about
it, she refused even to watch on TV.

"You should be ashamed," she told me.

"Why?"

"You're taking advantage of his need to perform. You may be sorry when it's over. He's not the Flying Wallenda."

She tried to talk Sterling out of doing it but he only kidded her back, and she finally got mad and hung up on him.

Then he had a fight with Mother Bogle, which I witnessed. For several months she had been allowing him to pay her rent in San Juan Capistrano as partial compensation for the gift of life, but recently, as part of his revelation, he'd decided he'd better concentrate on paying his own. So Loretta was back to depending on the money Denny made robbing homes and selling drugs. Lester hadn't been back for two years, although he had called Loretta periodically and had sent Sterling threatening cutouts from various cities. We later learned that he spent most of this period in one of those Western counties that has its own military.

I was at Sterling's apartment one afternoon, having brought over some Art Klee commercials he'd requested for study, when Loretta arrived to upbraid him for letting the team down financially. Her face, and Denny's, materialized suddenly in the kitchen window and made me jump. Sterling seemed used to it.

Denny waited outside, as usual, while Mrs. Bogle came in, with Dixie in her arms. She put the dog down and raised a burly fist toward Sterling.

"You're not too big for a mother to tap," she growled. "I've tapped Lester a few times."

"You can tap away," said Sterling, "but I don't have any money to spare right now."

Mother Bogle challenged this statement.

"You told me on the phone you were gonna do this big stunt. How much do you get for it?"

"If I do it right, I get my self-respect."

"Don't sass me, Vinnie. Denny's car is on its last legs. He predicts a complete breakdown this weekend."

"You want me to buy Denny a car."

"Well, it costs so much to fix, it makes more sense to just get another."

Sterling took a deep breath, and rubbed his face.

"I've been thinking about you and me," he said, "and things. Like names. I used to not like mine, when I was in school. But I got used to it. And I do my work with that name, Sterling Fleger. So . . . I think it'd be generous of you to try to think of me more that way."

Mother Bogle's chin quivered once, but she rallied. Looking at me, she shoved a thumb at Sterling.

"Actors," she said. To him, she continued, "You can call yourself Mr. Victor Mature, long as you do for the family."

"Well, about that . . . ," said Sterling.

Mrs. Bogle's eyes widened in alarm.

"I've given that some thought too," he said doggedly, "and I, I guess I owe you something. So, I'll send you a percentage of my pay, when I get any. Ten percent, same as my agent."

I have to say here, although you may think me cold, that I didn't think he should commit himself to a payment plan for this woman, and I thought ten percent was too much anyway, but he waved me off when I started to speak.

"Aside from that," he told her, "I think we should go back more toward the way we used to be."

"What way?"

"Well . . . seeing each other less."

She was shocked. Then she became hurt, and then furious. She turned to me.

"Was this your idea?" she demanded.

"It's mine," said Sterling. "I need for my life to be more— I need to be more . . . one guy or the other. And the one I've decided to lean toward being . . . is the one I'm used to."

"So. We're not good enough for you. Mr. Special."

She toured the room. Her eyes glittered.

"Ten percent. For the first year of your life, I gave a hundred percent or you wouldn't have lived. You had a soft spot on your head that went in and out like a volleyball."

Now it was Sterling's turn to look a bit alarmed, and I know what he was concerned about. He was wondering how many *times* it went in and out like a volleyball.

"I wonder why I made the effort," she continued, her voice trembling. "Why I went through the heartbreak to see you'd be taken care of. And why I kept a picture of a little baby all these years. So he could turn around and *kiss me off*."

She walked toward him slowly, looking so enraged and menacing that Sterling and I and Dixie all backed up.

"Ten percent of what? Money you won't make, or tell us if you've got it. All right. I see where I stand. He thinks he's better than us, doesn't he, Dixie. He thinks he's so special. Well, bite down on this: you're Vinnie Bogle. And ten percent of your acting is ten percent of shit. DENNY!"

As she wheeled and made for the door, I went for the steak knives, but she didn't want Denny to enter; she just wanted him to escort her and Dixie to the car. About fifteen seconds after storming out, she suddenly reappeared in the kitchen doorway and stood silent for a moment, looking defiant.

Finally she said, "Denny says you meant net."

Sterling said, "No, I meant gross."

"Oh," she said gruffly.

Then she left again.

It looked as though the stunt would be easy to promote. Elston's idea struck people as a vivid resolution of the issue: Could a baby safety suit withstand what would otherwise be a fatal impact? If it could, it would prove itself a fine product. And if not, it would still be good TV.

Art Klee taped an infomercial to run for a half hour prior to midnight on New Year's Eve. In it, he wore the deluxe suit, and used my line: "I know this suit'll protect *your* baby, 'cause I'm just a big baby myself." I was proud.

He also discussed the stunt in a taped interview for "Who's Hot/Who's Not," one of the entertainment TV newsmagazines. In the interview he said he'd love to make the flight himself, but he was already obligated to attend a conflicting New Year's celebration with Howard Stern. He revealed in closing that his place would be taken—and his lines spoken—by an old colleague from "Manhattan Live" whose career had been sidetracked by an amusing fluff, and then he told all about it. And that was the first the world ever really heard of Sterling.

The "Who's Hot/Who's Not" staff thought it was a cute story, and they unearthed a tape of the old Charles Manson bit to add to Klee's sound bite. Then they came over to the office and shot Sterling posing in the suit in front of Elston's office. Sterling was quietly thrilled, quite proud and didn't know the context in which he was appearing until the night the segment aired.

First came the chat with Klee, then the old, faded "Manhattan Live" tape of Sterling in his blindfold, shocking Klee and demolishing the Manson bit, and finally Sterling standing in the suit, with this voiceover:

"You'll see more of Sterling Fleger live at midnight on New Year's Eve—live, that is, if he survives his flight, his landing and his two lines of dialogue for the Little Spudge-Face Baby Safety Company."

I didn't call him up after the show.

The consensus at the office next morning was that it had all been good fun and even better publicity. Claire Simon loved it. "Now people are gonna *care,*" she said. "They'll want to see what happens. More viewers."

Elston was vaguely uneasy about this line fluffing talk. He had bought the airtime on the Parents cable channel, and now that he was committed to the buildup and the stunt, he was counting the things that could go wrong.

"Is your brother going to blow his lines?" he asked me that morning.

"That's the last thing you have to worry about," I told him.

Sterling and I had a lunch date that day. I saw him walk through the outer doors at twelve-thirty and came out of my office to meet him in the reception area.

"You okay?" I said.

"Yeah," he said. He seemed contemplative. He walked slowly up to the full-length wall poster of Art Klee we kept there in reception, and regarded it thoughtfully.

I laughed, a little laugh.

"Bet you pitched a fit when they showed that bit," I said. "Want to sue the show?"

"Nope," said Sterling quietly, looking Klee's picture up and down. "It's all true."

"Well, good," I said quickly. "That's the right attitude. It's not that big a deal. Claire says it enlists sympathy for you, and it builds suspense, so it's good, really. I mean, really."

Sterling nodded, still focused on the poster.

"I know what Lester would do," he said.

CHAPTER FOURTEEN

Claire Simon took full-page ads in papers in Los Angeles, Chicago, New York, Boston, San Francisco, Philadelphia, Denver and Miami, and even in *TV Guide,* announcing that the Little Spudge-Face Baby Safety Suit would demolish all criticism at midnight on New Year's Eve. There was artwork with it, showing a man in the suit blasting out of the mouth of a cannon, and indicating a trajectory that would have him landing on the sidewalk in front of the Siegfried and Roy billboard. Sterling's name was mentioned. His agent, Cubby McIlvaine, had insisted that the name Sterling Fleger be included in all print advertising.

Elston arranged accommodations for the Spudge-Face team at the Majestic Towers in Las Vegas for December 30 to January 2. Abby, Maggie and I were to get a suite across from Sterling, who was to get one all to himself. The prospect of staying at the Majestic Towers cheered him up considerably. They have a big sports book there, on the third floor—a huge room where you can sit and bet on every horse race in America and watch them all on your own little TV and get free drinks brought to you by women in shiny, skimpy costumes. It's kind of like the Dogpark for gamblers. Sterling had been there once during his intense handicapping period, and was looking forward to revisiting it after he got the stunt out of the way.

Since he spent all his time brooding over his lines and ignoring the possibility that he wouldn't live to say them, I took it upon myself to attend one of the test shoots conducted inland, near Murrietta Hot Springs, by Chad Mantle and his crew in early December. Chad was set up on a small section of flatland that equaled the length of the Strip that Elston had chosen for the demonstration. He had a cannon from the Hardy-Harrell Circus; he had a special effects supervisor and a stunt coordinator; he had all of Sterling's physical stats, and his dummies were the same dimensions and wore exactly what Sterling would wear. Chad distributed the weight in them in such a way that they assumed a Sterling-like stance through their trajectory.

On the afternoon I visited, Chad walked with me out to the end of the short runway in the desert in the sun and wind. Then we turned and faced the cannon, at the other end, and they loaded a Spudge-Face dummy into the muzzle.

Chad, a tall, lanky guy with hair over his eyes, waved toward the cannon.

There was a boom, and this tiny object sailed toward us in a high arc, getting bigger, flailing, descending faster and faster and landing—fwump—abruptly, awkwardly, legs crumpled, face forward, on the flat concrete target at our feet.

Chad squinted at the grotesque, twisted limbs.

"Thus it will always be," he said, "for those who break the code of *omerta*."

I stared at him.

"That's gonna be Sterling?"

Chad waved me off.

"Nah, that's what happens if you don't do anything in flight. He's gonna do something."

"Has Elston seen this?"

"Sure. He comes out every couple days, stands on that rock over there and goes, 'Activate the blister units!' He loves all this wowie-zowie show biz crap."

"Listen, Chad. That dummy is gonna be my brother."

"Ahh, he'll be all right. He just needs to be checked out on the accessories. Like his utility belt, you know? The basic blister unit apparatus operates automatically, but he's looking at such a heavy impact that he's got to manually increase that activity, he's got to pull a tab on the suit that double-puffs it . . . sort of jacks up his padding from astronaut size to Pillsbury Dough-Boy. See, the deluxe model has that feature. But he doesn't want to do it right out of the muzzle or he'll ruin his trajectory. It's not that tricky, though."

"So he's gonna be all right?"

We watched as the stunt coordinator and one

of his assistants dragged the dummy off the concrete and went over it for damage. Chad shrugged.

"Hell, yeah."

We had our dress rehearsal in mid-December. Sterling spent a few days before it wearing the suit in his living room, fiddling with the tabs, snaps and zippers and saying "Didn't hurt" and "How's your little Spudge-Face?" in as many ways as there are. Claire and Elston had decided against any new lines or special material. Elston told me they wanted to retain the wording the public identified with the product, but I think it was because they were afraid Sterling would muff something new.

Elston, Claire and I went out to the desert and watched Sterling get into the cannon. Chad shot him into a net in order for him to get used to the sensation of hurtling out of the muzzle of an artillery piece.

You may not know how they shoot a guy out of a cannon; I didn't. It's really pretty simple: Down in the base of the barrel they compress this giant spring, and they put a little platform over it. Then when it's time to shoot the human cannonball, they release the spring and set off a simultaneous and completely unrelated charge to stimulate the audience with a big boom.

I wouldn't have gone into the gun unless Maggie's life depended on it, but Sterling was, after all, a stuntman. He slid feet-first right down the barrel, and moments later, with a deafening report, hurtled into the air in a great arc and landed dead center in the net, which was suspended between poles about a city block from the cannon.

When he clambered out of the net, he shot both fists up in the air.

Elston, watching, said, "Let's try it at a higher elevation. Less distance, more height, so he can use the optional feature."

"I want to see him do the double-puffs," said Claire.

"The manual blister units," Elston corrected mildly.

Elston and Chad got into a low-decibel argument about when Sterling should double-puff—at three seconds out of the muzzle, or four.

Sterling joined us, striding over in the suit, and stood listening for a few moments, watching them through his helmet. Then he flipped his visor up and said, "I thought it was a *baby* safety suit."

"Baby and child," said Elston. "So?"

"Well, a baby wouldn't know to pull the tab to puff everything out further."

Chad Mantle looked nettled. "A baby isn't going to find himself in this situation," he said.

"For the purposes of this demonstration," said Elston, "you're using the deluxe model, which has this feature. A baby would need someone to pull the tab *for* him, but an eight-and-older child can do it himself."

Sterling thought that over.

"Okay," he said, and went off to prepare for his second flight.

This time Sterling counted to three one-thousand and double-puffed at the top of his arc. It was impressive. His velocity decreased as the suit blistered, bubbled and expanded in a rotating sequence; he began a spiraling descent while the suit ballooned like a popcorn bag in a microwave, and he landed buoyantly on an airbag the stunt coordinator had set up short of the net. By the time he hit, he was almost spherical.

I was reassured. The surface of the Las Vegas Strip would be considerably harder, but as long as he didn't land on his head—and Chad said the suit was weighted in such a way that he couldn't—he figured to survive.

You could see Elston felt vindicated. Like the safety suit, he too expanded, inhaling mightily, standing there beside Claire Simon.

Chad Mantle and I went over by the stunt coordinator to meet Sterling as he rolled out of the airbag.

"Deflate with the wrist bulb," Chad commanded.

Sterling squeezed a rubber attachment that extended from under his left sleeve into his palm, and the suit slowly shrank back to standard size. He then stood and removed his helmet. He looked bright-eyed, and good as new.

"So all you have to do," said Chad, "is wait for deflation, then walk over to your mark and say whatever."

Sterling, who had been smiling, lost the smile and gave Chad a steely glare.

"What's that supposed to mean?"

"What?"

" 'Say whatever.' "

"Whaddya mean?"

"I'm not going to say 'whatever.' I'm going to say two specific lines."

Chad shrugged.

"Whatever," he said.

Sterling's eyes widened. By this time Chad was behind him, unzipping the back of the suit and talking with Gary, the stunt coordinator.

"He's baiting me," Sterling muttered to me.

"No, he isn't. Have some Gatorade. Lighten up."

"I'm not gonna say 'whatever.' "

When Maggie was three, we got a Siamese kitten and named her Topaz. Topaz and Maggie adopted each other. I'd go into Maggie's bedroom the last thing at night to check on her and there they'd be, asleep together, Topaz's face in Maggie's hair.

Topaz was an indoor cat, but she got outside one day when she was about a year old and we lost her. The house we rent is up against the hills on the outskirts of town, and every night you can hear the coyotes, asking if the neighborhood's domestic animals can come out to play. They like to eat cats, and as the days passed and Topaz didn't come back, we had to assume they'd got her, although we didn't say so in front of Maggie.

We got another kitten for her, and she liked it, but one night about a week after Topaz disappeared, Maggie was taking her bath while I monitored from the living room, and I heard her crying. I went into the bathroom and she was sitting there in the water with the tears rolling down.

"What's the matter, honey?"

"Topaz used to watch me."

Abby had put out fliers all over the neighborhood offering a reward for the return of the cat, but there'd been no response. As a last kind of hopeless gesture, she put out new fliers specifying $300 as the amount. Whereupon an enterprising guy a few streets over put out food and a box trap and caught Topaz after *two weeks,* if you please. And she wasn't even skinnier; she'd been eating a lot of garbage and hiding in a tiny nook under a pile of lumber in the guy's side yard. Her only scars were emotional; she was relieved to be home, but she never really laughed it up after that.

I was lucky enough to be present, in our living room, when Maggie got the news that Topaz had been found. She lit up like the end of a musical, jumped off the couch and declared, "This is the first day of my life!"

This is now a family expression signifying extreme satisfaction, and Sterling used it on Christmas Day to describe his expectations for New Year's. He anticipated being reborn when he said his lines right. It disturbed me to hear him laying himself open like that.

He spent Christmas morning with us, as he had for several years. He enjoyed watching Maggie. Aside from being fond of her anyway, he liked to study her, since at such times her emotions were clearly visible on her face, undiluted by self-consciousness, and Sterling always filed that kind of thing.

He was a bit manic this Christmas, from nerves

and anticipation. He remarked again that his lines seemed uninspired. "How did you get all that emotion into 'Blah Blah Blah'?" he asked Abby. "That was great. I still remember that. I have to recover the freshness."

He looked huge in our living room, trying to step over Maggie's opened presents without squashing any. He couldn't sit still, and he couldn't stop talking about various aspects of the stunt. I'm pretty sure he wasn't on any drugs; he was just sizzling. When I challenged him to talk about something else, he said, "I bet Val comes back afterwards."

Abby told him he was putting too much weight on one part: "In the group we learn to spread that anxiety out a little, not give too much importance to any one performance."

Sterling gave no indication of having heard.

"Know what I like about your place, Age?" he said as he traded packages with Maggie. "It's like little-boy Christmas instead of big-boy Christmas."

He was referring to our Tall Paul Fleger Christmases from about age ten to seventeen, which were failures. We'd start out with a beautiful tree and presents beneath, and a turkey dinner planned for later. But somewhere during the opening of the presents everything would go straight to the ninth circle of hell. Mom would usually be mad at Dad for something he'd done the night before, and would react accordingly at the crucial, tense, expectant moment when he'd hand her the package designated "To Mom from Dad." She'd take the gift— a sweater or whatever—from its package, examine it briefly, toss it aside and say something like

"Hmph." That would be sufficient to send him off to the cabinet for an early bracer, and by noon we'd all look like we were in one of those earthquake drills they have at the schools out here. We never actually got to where you sit down at the dinner table. Customarily the turkey would be abandoned in the kitchen, and we'd sneak down individually during the night to sample it.

I made up my mind back then that if I survived to have a family of my own, we'd do Christmas more conventionally. So now with Maggie, we do it the Zane way, with presents in the morning and Abby's parents in the afternoon and a meal in there, usually around five. It lacks the intensity of the old days, but it's still an exciting novelty to me. Abby and Maggie do decorations.

"This ain't how the Flegers used to eat turkey," said Sterling as we sat down to dinner with the Zanes.

Abby had had an offer from a small label—Splendid Wren—to record an album of standards and we all talked about that at dinner. Abby's Dad, Ray, said he'd never heard of Splendid Wren, and Abby's mother told him he was an ignoramus.

"Any money in it?" asked Ray, a bulky, affable guy who was in the Kiwanis and ran a big patio furniture store.

"Not much," said Abby.

"Then you can sing what you want," said Sterling.

"I have an urge to cover this old Harold Arlen song called 'Now I Know,'" said Abby. "Dinah

Shore sang it. You don't get much more uncool than that."

"Do it anyway," said Sterling. "At the Actors' Bunker I get to do all kinds of stuff and it's great, even if it is for an audience of ten."

"You know," Ray Zane said to him, "if you're scared about talking on television, you ought to join Toastmasters International. They teach you how to get up and speak before any kind of crowd."

Sterling smiled into his plate. Then he chuckled, and scraped his chair back.

"Okay," he said.

"Where you going?" I asked him.

"I don't have to listen to that," he said.

"What did I say?" asked Abby's dad, as Sterling left the room.

Abby and I went after him and caught him as he was stacking his presents to go out the door.

"Hey," I said. "Go back in the kitchen, take the broom out of your ass and sit down."

Abby raised a hand to quiet me.

"Sterling," she said, "he didn't mean anything. He saw that stupid thing on 'Who's Hot/Who's Not.'"

Sterling nodded.

"Thinks he's talking to somebody who can't go off the low diving board," he said.

"No," said Abby. "He just loves that public speaking group. He got a certificate for a half-hour talk about his trip to Japan."

"Ster," I said, "your antenna is out too far."

He walked to the front door and turned as Mr. and Mrs. Zane came into the living room.

"I know what you're all thinking," he said, "and I don't have to stay around here and watch you all thinking it."

Whereupon he walked out, with his new watch and his new edition of Halliwell's *Filmgoer's Companion*.

"That's how the Flegers eat a turkey," I told Abby.

If you've gotten the idea that by this point Sterling was hypersensitive, then I've done my job as a reporter. He was vibrating like a giant hummingbird. I couldn't really blame him, though. He had one hundred percent of his self-esteem riding on New Year's Eve.

The day after Christmas he got two calls from old college chums who'd seen the print ad in *TV Guide,* saying they'd be watching, and the rest of the "gang" would be watching. There are few things that drive a man more than the need to impress the people he went to school with, especially if those people have written him off for years.

Val Fassero also called and wished him luck, just as a friend.

He finally couldn't stand it in Orange County anymore and left for Las Vegas on the 27th, a few days before the rest of the Spudge-Face crowd. He told me he wanted to walk the ground he'd be covering in flight, and in particular to stand in front of the Majestic Towers and say his lines.

I understood his reasoning. He felt he hadn't prepared sufficiently for that sketch on "Manhattan Live," and he wasn't going to make that mistake again. But there's such a thing as over-rehearsing. It was only seven words. He'd already said them so often they'd turned into sludge. I wished that instead of chanting the damn lines he'd take advantage of the distractions the town had to offer.

There are aspects of Las Vegas to criticize, but they've all been touched on so often that I don't have anything to add. Besides, I'd feel hypocritical because I like it there. Abby and I go about once every two years. It's lively. It's bright. You get a great deal on prime rib. They have free drinks if you gamble too, although I limit myself to Diet Pepsi.

I'm certain that if I'd gone to Las Vegas when I was still single and drinking, I'd have wound up on the street in the old part of town. It's all too much of a bargain for someone like I was. Nowadays I have my wife and my sobriety coins to protect me.

But I thought that for a day or two it might be just the ticket for Sterling. Kind of turn his thinking around so he could look at the trip as more of a vacation and less of a trial.

I called his suite the night he got there and he didn't answer. I thought that was good—that maybe he was in the sports book or at a topless vice den or somewhere like that. But when he called back, all he spoke of was how he'd paced off the distance of the shot, paralleling it, on the sidewalk, and how he was exercising to maintain his cardiovascular system. He was spraying his throat with Chloraseptic and sucking on vitamin C orange drops. He was swabbing his face with Sea Breeze to forestall any last-minute blemishes. It was all pretty clinical.

Elston and the rest of the Spudge-Face gang, along with our families, flew out en masse on the evening of the 29th. On the plane out of John Wayne Airport Abby came up with a word I hadn't heard anyone say since junior college.

"Hubris," she said. "Overreaching pride. Your boss up there in first class has it. He could've just tested the suit under everyday conditions. He didn't have to react this way. He could wreck his own company."

"I thought you were for it."

"Well, I don't know, now."

"Have a dream?"

"What if I did? It's still hubris, whether I had a dream or not."

"Well," I said, "Elston thinks big, honey."

"That's what I'm saying."

"We wouldn't be here if he didn't."

"That's what I'm saying."

"What I mean is, we wouldn't have had our first success if he didn't think like that."

We read our magazines for a few minutes. Joanne Petty came back into coach and walked past us to talk to a flight attendant.

"Any change in the tally?" I murmured to Abby.

"Shhh. I don't know. Why?"

"No reason, it's just that ever since you told me, I can't look at her without seeing this big 3."

"And what do you think of when you look at me?"

"Well, you know. Rainbow's end."

Joanne went past on her way back to first class, and our conversation returned to Abby's original point.

"Why doesn't he at least let Sterling land on one of those airbags?"

"It wouldn't be impressive that way. They are gonna carpet the street, though."

"Thick pile?"

"Look. If the suit works like it should, Elston'll look great, Sterling'll look great, people will know the suit's great, and we'll all be in the peach orchard."

"And what if Sterling lands in a heap and breaks?"

"Was that your dream?"

"No, in my dream it was Maggie."

"Well, Chad Mantle says he won't."

"But what if he does?"

I considered it for a moment.

"He won't have to say his lines."

CHAPTER FIFTEEN

I'm getting now to Sterling's big scene, some of which you probably saw on the news. There was a lot you didn't see, however; for instance, Sterling before the launch, and the full mix of onlookers in attendance that night.

I don't go out much on New Year's Eve anymore. Abby and I generally celebrate privately. But this time my presence was required outside the Majestic Towers, amid the whoop and holler. Claire Simon was going to be stationed across the street from the hotel, with the camera crew taping the stunt, and I was expected to stay with Elston and implement any spontaneous ideas he had.

The Las Vegas Strip is usually pretty packed with pedestrians in the evening. Many of the casinos are within walking distance of one another, and on a weekend there's quite a bit of surging back and forth.

On this night there was a huge extra turnout, especially around the Majestic Towers. Everyone who wasn't gambling or at a show was milling around outside, waiting for the countdown. The atmosphere was festive and noisy, but not as rowdy as you might expect; there was nobody knocking the newspaper vending machines over or climbing the sides of the buildings. Everybody seemed more anticipatory, I would say. They lined the roped-off section of street leading up to the hotel. The street was also lined at intervals by cops and a few able-bodied members of the Majestic Towers staff.

I was privileged; I got to walk under the ropes and onto the carpeted street itself. I didn't do it just to act important; I wanted to feel the rug Sterling would be landing on. It was burgundy, and it was thin. There wasn't a whole lot of give between it and the concrete. I had asked Elston to have them insert a layer of foam padding underneath, and they had. It didn't seem to make that much difference.

Elston gave interviews until eleven-thirty over by the cannon, which was about a block and a half down from our hotel, in the middle of the road, overseen by Chad Mantle and his staff. Gary the stunt coordinator and the special effects guy were there too, to oversee the placing of the charge in the cannon and to make sure Sterling was properly out-fitted. There was, however, no Sterling, at least not at 11:30 P.M., when the prerecorded infomercial featuring Art Klee began on the Parents channel.

After a final word to Chad Mantle about the

wind, Elston strode up the carpeted street to the landing site in front of the hotel, and I accompanied him. He wore a fawn-colored overcoat over his dinner jacket, and stroked his mustache downward repeatedly. We both waved up at the eleventh-floor Majestic Towers balcony, where Abby, Maggie and Bruyana Petty were looking down on the spectacle. The kids had been allowed to stay up to watch, but we'd all agreed they should be off the street. From Abby's vantage point the crowd made a big horseshoe shape, with the two ends pointing up the street toward the cannon and most of the people massed at the base, in front of the casino.

"Where's your brother?" Elston asked through a smile as he waved. "I haven't seen him since dinner."

"I saw him a couple hours ago. He was gonna rest up in his suite and take a last pee before he came down."

"Go get him."

My first shock of the night, as I walked across the street to the hotel to see what was keeping Sterling, was to walk spang into his old mate, Lee Ann, standing on the curb, scanning the sky.

She seemed taller, somehow, and gaunter than ever, like Mick Jagger in a light blue tailored robe/ gown and surrounded by several other people dressed in the same style.

"Lee Ann," I said.

She looked down at me haughtily, without recognition.

"It's me—A.J.—Beaver Fleger," I said. "Sterling's brother."

She nodded, briefly acknowledging me. I looked from her to her group.

"You're here to see Sterling do his stunt?" I asked.

"No," said a guy beside her. "We're here to see this entire town engulfed in flames while we ascend to sit before the Lord."

I nodded back repeatedly. I never know how to respond to that kind of thing.

"Got everything you need?" I asked finally.

"Worry about yourself," said a guy behind her. "It happens at midnight."

I looked at this fellow, and the other people by whom Lee Ann was surrounded.

"Bet you can't wait," I said to her.

She looked at me with a flicker of interest.

"It's no joke," she said. "Even you people know we're at the crisis. Otherwise why the armor? But you can't shield yourself from what's coming."

I nodded again and checked my watch.

"Well . . . ," I said.

"You think we're fools?" she asked.

"I can't really give an informed opinion, Lee Ann, I gotta—"

"Listen, you were always a nice kid, try to concentrate," she said, putting her hand on my arm with some urgency. Her eyes were dark and deep, back in her head. "This experiment is over. Do you think we're making progress? Do you think they're"—she swept a backhand gesture at the crowd—"making an effort? They aren't. They're as vicious as ever—more so, because they've got the technology. Do you know how many gunshots have been fired in American films since 1927?"

"How many?" I asked, curious.

"And how many *more* since *1990*?"

Lee Ann looked like she hadn't slept or sham-
pooed in quite a while, and was more raggedy than
I remembered her. On the other hand, I thought, if
you expect the world to end momentarily, you don't
worry about maintenance. You smoke 'em if you
got 'em. You don't floss.

"It only makes sense this way," she said. She
was trying to persuade me. She wasn't pleading; I
don't think Lee Ann would ever have done that . . .
but she seemed anxious for me to comprehend.

"I've looked at this from every angle," she said.
"It only makes sense if you approach it sociotheo-
logically. *Then* you see that Revelations anticipates
the present power structure. It's that *structure* that's
the Antichrist. Otherwise"—she gestured to include
the street, the town, the world—"it's all just a bad
joke, and I won't accept that. I won't accept all this
bullshit and evil. I'm going. These people are going.
And I'm not making it up. It's written; it's just been
mistranslated."

She had more, but I don't remember it. Sometimes you run into someone with a torrent of words
to offer on some subject and you've got other com-
mitments and you can't retain it.

"I gotta go too, Lee Ann. I gotta find Sterling."

"I'm trying to save you both."

"How about afterwards?"

"There isn't going to *be* any afterwards. You
think I've repudiated my intellect, but I haven't, I've

studied this. I'd've translated it from the Aramaic if that were possible."

"I'm sure you've done your homework, but if I don't get Sterling, and the world *doesn't* end, I'm screwed. It's good to see you again."

As I walked on, I heard her calling after me, "You say you're protecting babies and you demonstrate it by shooting off a gun."

I made my way through the people milling around outside the Majestic, and went in, through the ground-floor casino to the elevators.

Sterling was up in his suite on the eleventh floor. He had the suit on. He was standing in his living room area.

"The hell's goin' on?" I asked him. "C'mon."

His visor was up, so I could see his face, which was ghastly.

"Okay," he said. "I'm just a little hot and cold."

He collapsed onto the couch, and I scrambled to get him into a sitting position. The skin of his face was clammy. His eyeballs were fluttery. He smiled weakly.

"I don't let just anybody see me like this," he said.

"What is going on? You look like the hotel stationery."

"A little sweaty is all. Gotta put my face on some tile."

I snapped the helmet off and he crawled to the bath area, where he lay facedown beside the circular tub.

There was a knock on the door to the suite.

When I looked through the little eyehole I saw Abby and the kids, so I opened it and let them in. Abby turned on the TV for the kids and then came with me to the bath area, where we stood over Sterling.

"You look sick," I told him.

"Doesn't matter," he said.

"He's right," said Abby.

I stared at her. "*You're* pretty tough."

"He's gotta do it," she said flatly.

Sterling turned his head to cool the other side of his face on the floor.

"I don't know why everybody's making such a big deal," he said. "I'm fine."

"You say that," I replied, "but you're lying on your nose."

He swallowed diligently, once or twice, and spoke quietly. He seemed to prefer to say words that didn't require him to move his lips.

"Shouldn't have shown off with the lobster."

"What's the matter, what've you got?"

"Normal pregame jitters; maybe a little cholera."

Right about now you may be saying to yourself, This lad isn't cut out for the stage. But what it was, was he just had this one specific weak spot, and that's not unheard of in the annals of show business. For instance, Clark Gable, Grandma Jessie's old favorite, wouldn't do the Jack Benny radio show because he was afraid he'd blow chunks at a live microphone. And he was a tough guy.

So, looked at from a certain angle, that makes Sterling braver than Clark Gable, because here he was at least trying to get up and perform, even though he'd apparently been losing weight from both ends for the last hour or so.

He now made motions as if to rise, and I helped him back to the living room, where I picked up his helmet.

"Let's don't put that on yet," he said.

He sat on the couch. Maggie came up and stood in front of him while Bruyana continued watching TV.

"The hat's hot, isn't it," she said sympathetically.

"It's all right," said Sterling.

"If you're nervous, you can do like my brave summer."

Last August Maggie got back on a pony after she fell off, and she took swimming lessons, and she played a little song on the keyboard at a local kids' talent show, all despite declarations that she couldn't and wasn't going to, so we had called it her brave summer.

"Okay, sweetie," said Sterling, and gestured for us to get her away from him. "I don't wanta, y'know"—he flopped his hand forward, palm up—"in front of her," he murmured.

Abby took the kids back across the hall, then reappeared in the doorway.

"Did you take some Imodium?" she asked.

Sterling nodded.

"Remember what we say in FA," said Abby. " 'God grant me the serenity—' "

" '—not to soil my pants,' " they finished together. He nodded again, and she left, crossing the hall and shutting her door.

Sterling rose, walked to the bathroom sink, poured water on his face and gargled some Plax. Then he looked at himself in the mirror and said, "He ha ho hoo."

I sensed a figure in the doorway and looked over, thinking it was Abby again, but I was wrong. It was Lester.

He wore a gray, hooded UNLV sweatshirt and carried a black duffel. He'd gotten heavier in hiding. He was still beady-eyed and mad. I never saw him when he wasn't.

He was in a hurry, too. His eyes flicked past me to the bathroom, where he spotted Sterling.

"You look like Captain Pussy in that suit," he said.

Sterling saw Lester in the mirror, blinked slowly, lowered his head and shook it.

"I don't have much time," said Lester briskly, dumping his duffel on the lamp table and rummaging through it. "I have to get back to my unit."

"You're in the army?" I asked, incredulous.

"I'm in the one true American army, pissant," he said, producing a large manila envelope from the bag.

Sterling came out of the john and faced him.

I had to accept it, finally: They were brothers. Since neither of them could stand the sight of the other, they had similar expressions on their faces, so the resemblance stood out more. They had the same mouths, was the main thing.

"You're all the bitch talks about," said Lester, extracting some stapled pages from the envelope. " 'Watch your brother, he's gonna kiss his own ass on TV and give me ten percent.' Ten percent, ten percent, I hear it in my sleep. So the narc is the good son and I'm dirt. I was gonna just kill ya, but then I thought, no." He slapped the pages onto the table in front of Sterling. "You're gonna read that on TV."

Sterling picked it up, and I came and looked over his shoulder.

"It's your apology for that show, and for ratting me out to the cops," Lester went on, "and the rest of it's the new U.S. Constitution. I'm in Americans for a Brighter Day, we're gonna turn this country around."

Lester's document was hand-printed. The first page was Sterling's apology, and the next twelve were a kind of manifesto. I can't recall much of it because I always tend to click off whenever I see the word "mongrelization," but in general it expressed dissatisfaction with the present system and most of the people in it. It was stamped in blue at the end: "Americans for a Brighter Day."

Sterling nodded a few times as he turned the pages, then looked back up at Lester.

"You got an interesting outlook on history," he said. "Lemme ask you a historical question: Ever hear of Garland Bernard?"

"Yeah, I did. You're not so fuckin' smart."

"Who was he?"

Lester looked peeved; he didn't have time for this.

"I know the name. I don't have to answer trick questions. He invented the steamboat. Are you gonna read it or not?"

Sterling smiled and rubbed the paper gently between his fingers.

"Actually, you brought this just in time," he said, and indicated the bathroom. "I was having a TP crisis in there."

Lester's face went all bony, as it had on our previous meeting. He went for Sterling's throat, and the three of us hit the floor together. Sterling managed to get an arm around Lester's neck from behind. Lester hawked and hissed, punching at me while I tried to thumb his eyes out.

We were interrupted as we grappled on the rug by two Majestic Towers staffers who had been sent upstairs by Elston to find Sterling. As they separated us, Lester scrambled to his feet, grabbed his duffel and ran out the door. I followed him into the hallway and saw him take the stair exit. Then I pounded on our suite door until Abby opened it. She was shocked at my expression.

"Honey," I said, "you're goin' in the vault."

There was no time to search for Lester; Sterling and I had to go downstairs. At our insistence, the Towers staff moved Abby and the kids to another room, three floors up. Then Sterling and I took the elevator down to the casino. While we descended, Sterling wiped some blood from under my nose with his glove.

"He can't find 'em," he assured me.

"He can find you," I pointed out. "He's mad at you."

"Ahh, he's halfway back to the swamp or the compound or wherever he lives. Besides, I got you looking out for me." He swabbed my face vigorously with his cuff, scraping my skin raw.

The elevator reached the ground floor and the doors opened. Sterling was about to step out, but then froze and turned pale again.

"Oh, shit."

"What?"

"Line."

I stared at him.

" 'Didn't hurt,' " I said.

He nodded, exhaled and started walking. Lester was forgotten. He was back in the world of flop sweat.

Moving slowly through the casino, we were the object of even the gamblers' attention. Sterling was striking, with his totally pale face topping the Baby Safety Suit ensemble. I kept looking this way and that for Lester. Sterling kept his eyes front.

We made it past the tables and the check-in desk. He stopped as we reached the glass street doors. His face had a slick pallor.

"You okay?" I asked.

"Val's out there," he said.

I looked through the glass and saw nothing but strangers.

"How can you tell?"

"I can sense it. She's out there. I've got to pull myself together."

He took a deep breath.

" 'Twelve O'Clock High,' " he intoned, " 'is a Quinn Martin Production.' "

He pushed open the doors and lurched outside.

•　　•　　•

It was lit up like night baseball. Several giant searchlights pointed at the sky. The crowd lining the ropes consisted of a thousand or two tourist families and other, more unaffiliated types who had come out to welcome the clean slate. To our left, on the way to the cannon, were the the '96ers. Ahead of us, across the street, Claire's cameras were positioned at intervals to shoot Sterling's landing and his lines. Elston and Joanne Petty stood behind Camera C, the one Sterling would finally face. To our right, in the street, beyond the end zone, so to speak, since Sterling would be flying left to right, was the largest group of onlookers, of every age and contour. There was no sign of Lester.

We had to go to the left, past the '96ers, and I was glad of it, because when Sterling saw Lee Ann the shock straightened him up.

"There will be fire and a sword and the coming of the Father's Son," intoned somebody in Lee Ann's bunch as she and Sterling looked each other over.

"You look scared," said Lee Ann. "Losing your nerve?"

"I'd rather lose my nerve than my marbles," he replied, glancing at her companions.

"While you do this shabby circus act of yours," she said, "Jesus Christ will be descending."

"Hope we don't collide," said Sterling politely.

"Scoff," she nodded, "but take my advice: now is not the time to make a masturbatory display of yourself."

"Whaddya mean, masturbatory?" Sterling asked, genuinely surprised.

"Getting shot out of a cannon?" Lee Ann said. "Come on."

Elston Petty crossed the empty carpeted section of the street toward us as Sterling reacted with injured innocence to Lee Ann's accusation.

"*I'm* not masturbating," he retorted. "I'm the *sperm*. If anybody's masturbating around here it's *him*."

Elston now joined us to address Sterling with brusque anxiety.

"You belong over by the cannon," he said. "What's the matter, you're white as a sheet."

"He's the sperm," said Lee Ann.

Elston flicked a glance at Lee Ann, then stared intently into Sterling's eyes.

"Are you all right?" he asked.

"Sure," said Sterling.

"You're not concerned about the landing, are you?"

"He's not going to land," declared a tall young guy standing next to Lee Ann. "One day with God equals a thousand years for Man. God took six days to create the universe and then rested. That's six thousand years. Using 4004 B.C. as a date for the beginning of scripturally tabulated history, and adding 1996, that comes to six thousand. Time's up."

We all stared at this kid. He had a high forehead and one of those beards that only grow on the bottom of your chin.

"Son," said Elston finally, "you're a pinhead. And at 12:05, you'll know it." He took Sterling by the arm to lead him past the '96ers, but Sterling resisted, looking at Lee Ann.

"Hugs," he said. "Come on now. Last chance if you're right."

I would not have suggested "hugs" to Lee Ann, looking her most warlike, but Sterling's appeal moved her after all, and she allowed herself a farewell embrace for old times' sake.

Elston took me aside.

"What's wrong with him?" he hissed at me. "Why is he so sweaty?"

"He's just excited."

He looked back at Sterling, who was wiping his sleeve across his forehead as Lee Ann gave a thumbnail synopsis of her eschatological reasoning.

Elston quivered, as if he'd had a sudden chill.

"He's out," he said abruptly. "What's the stunt coordinator's name? We'll let him do it."

"What do you mean? Sterling's fine."

"Look at him. He's melting."

"He is *not*. He's hot in the suit."

"The suit is aerated!"

"Oh, bullshit, you wouldn't be hot in these lights in that suit?"

"For the practice shots he didn't turn a hair. Now he looks horrible."

"I've known that guy all my life," I said quietly. "You can't go by how wet he is. He will not let you down."

"You'd better be sure, A.J.," said Elston. He was quite calm suddenly. "I'm going to hold you responsible."

That's an interesting trait, isn't it, that bosses have. They get an idea. You say you don't like it. You end up responsible.

"If you're wrong," he went on, "I want you to be clear on the consequences. You won't just be destroying your career. You'll be subverting a great movement. If man is to have hope, he has to have beacons. A sense of climbing out of the muck. The Little Spudge-Face Company is a beacon."

He said some more to this effect, but I had gone off on a mental tangent when he said "destroying your career." My family's economic edifice stood on my Spudge-Face salary. I saw the future without that paycheck as clearly as if I were Mrs. Bogle's driver Denny: No rent payments. No other job. Abby back to office work. Entry level. No college for Maggie. No orthodonture. Homeless finally. Divorce. Abby and Maggie better off. No visitation. Back to Illinois. Men's room attendant.

"Stop pinching my shoulder," I told Elston. "He can do it. Let him do it."

Sterling joined us, dripping sweat, and said, "Let's do it before I get the shits again."

Elston closed his eyes.

"Elston, come on," I said. "They're gonna go three-two-one, and if you have a delay or a postponement you're gonna look like a wienie."

He said nothing.

"Go on, go back over there," I said. "You're on before we are."

He opened his eyes, glared at me fiercely, spun and walked away, across the carpet, to Claire and the Spudge-Face group ranked around the cameras at the landing area.

As we moved on toward the cannon, Sterling mumbled to himself. I assumed he was going over his lines. I was glad Lee Ann had distracted him, but I hoped she hadn't distracted him too much. A mental video popped into my head of him facing the camera and saying, "How's your little Sperm-Face?" This led me back into the sequence in which I became a men's room attendant.

"Got your character?" I asked.

"Characters," he corrected me. "For the 'Didn't hurt' I'm a happy toddler, and for the second line I'm a confident, friendly company spokesman."

"You want to run the lines?"

"I've said them too much already."

As we neared the big gun, people on both sides of the street hollered at Sterling ebulliently. The street was so bright, and the atmosphere so close to room temperature, that it began to seem odd to me; it felt as though we were indoors.

Sterling punched himself rhythmically in the chest with his clenched fist. He saw me looking.

"Trying to get a more regular heartbeat," he said.

I nodded. "That's good. Have fun with it."

At the cannon, Chad Mantle and the crew frisked him to make sure the suit was in working order. A reporter from *Buyer Beware* magazine was also present, at Elston's invitation, to make sure the safety features Sterling wore were identical to those in our deluxe model. I stared at the huge muzzle of the gun. It was smooth bore.

The digital clock jutting out from the wall of the nearby Pendleton Bank Building said 11:56. I looked at a TV monitor we had set up nearby. The infomercial was coming to a close, with a musical number featuring different-sized kids in the safety suit, jumping around on camera.

"Two or three minutes to the end of the show," I told Sterling, "then Elston and Claire do the intro up the street, they wave, we wave, countdown, boom."

"Remember to double-puff on three," Chad told him.

"I don't like using a feature a baby isn't smart enough to use," said Sterling.

"Pretend you're a prodigy," said Chad.

Sterling's eyes narrowed while Chad turned and supervised the lowering of the gun muzzle.

"Guy's always *dissin'* me," he muttered.

"He's just like that, forget it," I said.

I felt awkward. Twenty years earlier, just before his debut, I'd said something that unsettled him, so now I was inhibited. Now that another big moment had arrived and it was time for one of us to get in a cannon, I think we both felt uncomfortable. We looked up the street toward the hotel.

"Funny Lee Ann being here," said Sterling.

"Yeah."

"Well," he said, "pull yourself together, you look terrible."

The infomercial ended and Claire Simon and Elston appeared on the nearby monitor, welcoming the viewers to the Little Spudge-Face New Year's Baby Safety Suit Demonstration. When they turned our way, Sterling waved and climbed into the lowered mouth of the cannon, feet first. Then one of Gary's assistants cranked the muzzle up to the proper elevation, and Sterling, with his head and arms sticking out, looked down at me, his helmet visor up.

"Line," he called down.

"What?"

"The line. Start it."

"Don't do that."

"*Line.*"

I stared, and gave it to him.

"I knew it," he called. "I just wanted to make sure." He looked up the street and I saw his lips move as he muttered to himself.

The countdown began, signaled by the clock on the bank building and called out by the crowd.

On the count of six or five, Sterling disappeared into the muzzle of the cannon.

"*Didn't hurt,*" I called again.

It wasn't until he'd already gone down the gun barrel that I saw Valerie Fassero. She was on the left-hand side of the street, about halfway down, in a long green coat, hurrying through the crowd and looking back over her shoulder at the cannon, moving as if on punt coverage.

To my shock, I also saw Mrs. Bogle's Denny over by the '96ers, just seconds before the shot. He was kind of tangoing his way to the front of the group with his hands in his pockets, while Lee Ann and the others scanned the sky.

I couldn't quite assimilate that, because two seconds later everybody began screaming even louder than they already were, and there was a *Boom!* next to me, and Sterling went rocketing up into the starry night.

I started running, just inside the ropes on the left side of the street, toward the landing area. I wanted to get there in time to see him say his lines. I threw a glance upward as I went, to track his trajectory, and saw that his arc looked good. I experienced a momentary, irrational anxiety that he might explode, but dismissed it.

That fear was replaced by another as he sailed past the count of three one-thousand and didn't do what he was supposed to. As he reached the peak of his arc and began descending, I saw that his appearance wasn't changing enough. By that I mean that he puffed, but he didn't double-puff. The dumb bastard didn't pull the ring, the tab thing on his chest panel. He didn't even flap his arms.

I stopped running as he neared the ground and yelled at him; not any actual words, but a yell. But he didn't respond; he didn't do anything. He just sort of, I guess you'd say, depended on the basic suit as sold.

Consequently he carried farther than he would have if he'd fully puffed—almost into the crowd beyond the landing area, like a golf shot carrying the green.

People had been hollering constantly from a few minutes to midnight until now, but for some reason they seemed to subside just before he landed, so I swear, I heard him hit, on the far edge of the carpet. He landed forwardly, on his left side. He may have intended to roll, but he didn't. He bounced instead, and jackknifed. I said, "*Oh,*" on impact, a sympathy gasp.

I look back now and think I couldn't possibly

have heard him hit the ground from where I was. There was other noise, and distance . . . but in my memory, there *is* a sound, similar to what you might get if you threw a beanbag chair off your roof.

CHAPTER SIXTEEN

Sterling didn't soften his landing because

    A. He forgot.

    B. He felt it was out of character to do in a baby safety suit what a baby couldn't do.

    C. He chose to commit suicide so he wouldn't have to say his lines.

    As I ran toward him again, I thought maybe C. The feeling he'd developed about live TV over the last twenty years was deeper than the phrase "stage fright" is adequate to describe. It was conceivable that at the last moment he'd decided he'd rather die on impact than to face the glass eye.

    On the other hand, B was just as likely. Sterling had integrity as a performer; he hated to fuzz up his character. I know it had bothered him, that manual double-puff option, because he knew a baby couldn't use it, and neither could a toddler, which is what he was supposed to be when he said his first line. It was just possible he'd made one of those actor's choices he often spoke of.

As I ran up the street toward the heap on the carpet edge, I didn't really know why he hadn't cushioned his fall. But I thought it quite conceivable that he was dead. The basic Spudge-Face Safety Suit was a fine product, but Chad hadn't designed it to rewrite the statutes governing the high fall.

Sterling moved slightly, on the rug, kind of writhing, as I ran toward him, but it didn't soothe me. I assumed it was death throes.

But then he raised a hand, and I skidded to a stop. It occurred to me that he was probably still on camera, and that he knew it.

We had an ambulance nearby, of course. Sterling had jokingly requested a horse van, like at the track, so he could be humanely destroyed if necessary. The paramedics went toward him on the trot after he landed, but he waved them off as he struggled to one knee. They too paused and watched. We were about twenty feet from him.

The crowd in front of the hotel had moved forward too, but as Sterling forced himself to his hands and knees, they hesitated, and held back. I looked over at the Pettys and Claire Simon, and they were all frozen, staring at him.

I later found that Claire's number one cameraman had followed the flight up to and including the crash, then panned to Elston, and then went back to Sterling, figuring that of the two of them, Sterling looked better.

He finally stood, which in itself was a colossal

testimonial to the Little Spudge-Face Baby Safety Suit. I took it to be one of those things people do when they're mortally injured but have momentum going; I waited for him to sink back into a puddle. Instead, he slowly began moving toward his agreed-upon mark in front of Camera C. He took small steps, tilting from side to side like a windup toy. As he walked, he slowly raised one hand and released the visor tab, opening the helmet to reveal his face.

It was the happy, fresh face of a little kid.

It was amazing; I would have thought it impossible. He looked bright-eyed, lighthearted, pain-free and proud, as if he'd just put his shoes on the right feet for the first time. To see him smiling youthfully like that, with maybe three-fifths of his 206 bones broken . . . well, the tears just popped into my eyes.

I cried when Claire Danes died in *Little Women;* I was impressed when DeNiro got so fat in *Raging Bull*. But this was the finest performance I ever saw. Sterling was showing what I'd always thought he had—greatness. It was his character, overcoming everything.

I caught a movement to my left and saw that Valerie Fassero had stepped out from the crowd and was watching him from just inside the street rope. Her face was distorted. She looked as shattered as he was.

A few of the '96ers in front of the hotel had come forward a bit, dividing their attention between Sterling and the heavens. I heard the kid who'd told us the six-thousand-year theory ask Lee Ann, "That couldn't be Him, could it?"

"No," said Lee Ann gloomily. "That's my old boyfriend."

"Did we miscount?" asked somebody.

Sterling tottered on toward the camera, still wearing his carefree toddler's smile, and had almost reached his mark when a man came up behind him from the hotel side of the street. He wore a gray UNLV sweatshirt and carried a black duffel. He said, "I'm a doctor." Sterling waggled his right hand backward, waving him away without turning.

"Don't walk away from me," said Lester.

Sterling recognized the voice that time. He stopped and slowly managed to turn, and they faced each other, a few feet apart.

"Who *is* that?" hissed Claire Simon. "He's on camera."

I went forward in a semicircle, trying to stay off-screen myself.

"Lester," I murmured. "Sterling's busy."

Lester ignored me.

"Are you gonna read it?" he demanded.

With some difficulty, Sterling shook his head once.

"Okay," said Lester, nodding. "See Denny?"

We looked and spotted him among the '96ers near the hotel entrance, standing just behind Lee Ann. She saw us looking in her direction and turned to look at Denny too.

"I'm gonna show you what it's like to hurt," said Lester.

Sterling slowly swiveled his head to look at me, as if to say, "He's gonna show me what it's like to hurt."

"First you're gonna lose your girl," Lester went on.

This statement threw us a little. I stared at Lee Ann.

"She's not his girl," I said.

"Bullshit, we saw 'em together," said Lester.

"Who are you? What are you doing?" Lee Ann said distinctly to Denny, over by the curb. He said something I couldn't hear and moved the hand in his right coat pocket.

I walked past Lester and over toward Denny, who raised his pocket at me.

"You just hustle to do any dumb-ass thing the Bogles say, don't you?" I hissed at him.

"I see a couple separated," he replied, swami-like, "and me getting away in the confusion."

"She's not his girlfriend, stupid," I informed him. "You can't even see into the present."

"It's all right, let him do it," said Lee Ann, looking at his pocket. "I'm ready." She faced him. "C'mon, you little tick, whoever you are. Let's see you do it. C'mon."

Unnerved, Denny looked past me at Lester, who muttered, "Wait," and fished in his duffel. He seemed rattled by Lee Ann's attitude. "I'll say when."

"This is your big plan?"

The voice, low and raspy, was Sterling's, as he hobbled toward Lester. He had to be hurting bad, but he was mad enough not to care.

"This is it?" he said contemptuously. "You're the brains and Denny's your stooge? He whacks her while you talk big? Who are you supposed to be, Charlie Mans—"

He stopped and closed his eyes briefly. Then he turned and squinted at the camera, which was still focused on him. Finally he looked upward, as if calling on Jesus to come down and give him a break.

"Believe that?" he asked. "I said it again."

"Hey, I'm Lester *Bogle*," Lester reminded him, getting irate. "You don't like to hear that name. Bogle-Bogle-Bogle. The name you shat on."

The surrounding crowd stirred at that, but no one seemed to want to join us inside the ropes. There were traffic police present, but I can't really blame them for not taking over. The situation was ambiguous. Nobody had really done anything. It must have been hard to figure out what we were all talking about. They might have thought it was some kind of prep for a further demonstration. Also, there were bystanders on all sides.

Among them was Elston Petty, standing next to the cameraman and staring at all of us. He was a pillar. You could have stood him in the park.

Valerie Fassero was transfixed too, watching Sterling. She seemed poised to run into the street and comfort him, but I think that like Elston, she was still hoping he might get around to saying his lines.

Lester had worked himself up to a boil.

"I do what I have to do my*self*!" he said now. "I leave the heavy work to *me*! And I don't need some bush-league actor to do me, either. The next time they do a show about me, it won't be you in my part—it'll be fuckin' Harvey Keitel."

With that, he hollered, "Denny!" and went back to rummaging furiously through his duffel.

Denny's coat was flapping as he tried to wrestle his hand out of his pocket. I was closest to him, except for Lee Ann, so it seemed to be up to me.

I looked at the stars shining above the Majestic Towers. Then I kind of gasped and staggered sideways and pointed up. I did it the way I thought Sterling would have. Sterling's accent, with maybe some Richard Harris.

"Oh my God, Lee Ann, look. It's true. It's Him."

Lee Ann looked up. "Where?" she asked.

"The horse," I said. "Oh, God. The *sword*."

"Oh, right," said Denny skeptically. But seeing us both gaping upwards, he felt he had to check. I guess deep down, Denny lacked confidence in his own visionary powers. And he also probably lacked a certain minimum level of intelligence. So he took a look upward and I hit him in the Adam's apple.

The tempo of events accelerated after that. On the videotape you can see Lester coming up with the contents of his duffel. You can't see it very well, but of course it was a gun. It looked like the one Sterling used on "Open Cases," an assault rifle. I don't know what brand. The onlookers who saw it started yelling.

Sterling wobbled forward toward him. You can see by the way he's moving on the tape that he doesn't care about getting shot. He was already badly damaged anyway, and besides that he'd said "Manson" again. You can't hear it clearly, but he was cursing Lester vigorously. I was close enough to hear part of it.

"See, that's why you're such a fucking feeb, Lester," he said. "You don't know what's appropriate."

The only thing I recall Lester saying in reply was, "Think you're so special." This was the Bogles's battle cry. The Bogles were dedicated to making sure nobody thought he was special.

With Denny holding his windpipe and coughing and waving to indicate time out, I could see that Lester was by far the bigger threat, so I went for my rock.

I had one left. I'd discarded the others long before, since Lester hadn't shown up and they made my clothes lumpy. But I'd kept this shiny little flat gray one because I'd decided it was lucky. I now hauled it up out of my pocket and zinged it sidearm at Lester's head.

He was standing maybe fifteen feet away. The rock practically whirred, I threw it so hard. And that was my error, because if I'd held up just slightly I'd've had better control. As it was, it shot right in front of his face, past him, and hit someone in the crowd. It hurt her too, to judge by the outcry. I don't know who she was; I never saw her. I still feel bad about it. It illustrates the bystander problem we had, surrounded like that. When people tell me the police should have just started blazing away when they saw Lester with his gun, I refer them to what happened with my rock.

Lester saw the rock go by, traced its course backward and decided to shoot me first. He turned toward me, but Sterling lumbered forward and whapped the gun barrel down.

"That's my brother," he said.

You couldn't say this remark set Lester off, exactly—he was already set off—but it incensed him further. He wrenched the gun free and shot Sterling point blank in the chest.

Sterling was hurled backward and landed flat on the carpet.

People screamed, jostled and ran in all directions. Some big fleeing huckleberry knocked me to my knees.

I saw Sterling, on his back, raise an arm feebly, pull the ring on his chest and double-puff.

I thought, *Now* he does it.

Lester flinched and jumped back in alarm when Sterling began rolling, popping and expanding on the ground, but then he recovered and fired into the suit again. The suit and Lester's gun were both popping. Lester's features were clenched as he fired.

The cops had their weapons out but I didn't wait; I ran at Lester from a three-point stance and hit him waist-high from the side, taking him and his gun to the carpet. On the videotape I'm blurry, there in the zoom, but that's me, tackling Lester and then pummeling him. And the reason I stopped so suddenly—stopped hitting him—is that I noticed the front of his sweatshirt was getting bloody.

I don't recall if I mentioned that there were a few security guys in the green livery of the Majestic Towers out on the sidewalk. I think I did. Anyway, they'd had different training than the police had. They didn't worry so much about bystanders. They addressed themselves to first causes only. Seeing Lester, they looked no further.

What happened was that just as I tackled Lester, two of these gentlemen fired at him with their own weapons. In acting as they did, they displayed little concern for the people beyond us, across the street. It turned out later that their confidence in their aim was only half justified.

At the time, I was bewildered. I couldn't figure out what had happened. I'd been punching at Lester's head, and here he was blossoming blood on his lower shirtfront.

His face turned as pale as Sterling's had been in the hotel. He was shocked.

Somebody pulled me off him. The casino staffers and the police were around us. I have an impression of talking to Lester, but I don't remember what I said. You can't hear me on the tape because everybody was hollering at that point.

A police officer swung me around, and I saw some more cops disarming Denny fifty feet away. Lee Ann was still standing. The other '96ers had gathered around her.

I convinced the cop holding me that I wasn't going to attack anyone anymore and he relaxed his grip. Lester lay at my feet, his eyes bulging in panic. A couple of paramedics came up and squatted over him.

"Don't move," said one.

"I can't bend my knee," said Lester. "Fix it."

Then I saw that Sterling was still moving. He was rolling from side to side on his back, bug-like, gathering momentum in an effort to turn over. He

had squeezed the small hand-bulb attachment to deflate the blister units and was now back to basic
suit size.

As I watched him, he rolled over onto his hands
and knees. One of the paramedics reached down to
help and Sterling slapped at him.

I called to the paramedic, "Wait—he wants to
do something."

We all watched Sterling, all of the rest of us
who were still close by—Lee Ann and the '96ers;
the cops; the security guys; the paramedics who
weren't already attending to Lester; and Valerie Fassero.

He proceeded slowly, on an elevated crawl, toward the camera set-up. He stopped about six feet
away from it and made a little gesture for the cameraman to come in tighter on him.

Sterling looked up at the lens from his position
on his hands and knees on the edge of the carpet.
The camera stared back down at him. He smiled
and said,

"Didn't hurt."

Now I was there and I'm telling you: That was
acting. Don't come around me with your Nicholas
Cage; I'd like to see *any* other actor take an equiv-
alent amount of automatic weapons fire and match
that reading.

Sterling did the next line with a more mature
delivery:

"How's *your* little Spudge-Face?"

You'll notice: Each word right.

He maintained the smile, unblinking. I realized
he was going to hold it until he died or the camera

moved. I waved for the cameraman to pan to me and faced the lens as manfully as I could.

I said, "On behalf of the Little Spudge-Face Baby Safety Company, Happy New Year." They didn't show that on the news, though. I got left off.

While I was speaking, Sterling fell on his face and Valerie Fassero ran up and covered him like a tent. The paramedics joined her, and this time Sterling didn't protest or even move.

A moment later, Elston Petty sank to the street beside the camera, looking chalky and stunned. One of the shots from casino security had missed Lester and hit him. Claire Simon came back from the scattered crowd and bent over him, as did Joanne Petty.

He said, "I've been struck down."

It would turn out that the wound wasn't life-threatening; a security man's bullet had gone through Elston's side, tearing his left love handle.

But it distracted me briefly from watching the paramedics as they loaded Sterling onto his stretcher. When I looked back down at him—motionless, eyes closed, on his back in the safety suit—I felt a sudden conviction rising in me that now he really *was* dead—that he had done what he had to do and now his body had given up. I got a shock to my heart and burst into a sweat.

Bending down, I yelled at him over Val Fassero's shoulder:

"Ster! Ster! We didn't get it! You gotta do it over!"

He twitched.

"Kill you," he mumbled.

I don't know if he got it from the Bogles or the Flegers, but he was one tough actor.

That night, in bed at the hospital, with the Demerol level rising, Sterling told Valerie Fassero and me his theory of nature versus nurture, heredity versus environment. He was euphoric, although he would later come to realize that he had a staggering number of external and internal injuries to arms, legs, pelvis, sternum and spleen.

We didn't know if he was going to make it, so we listened to him closely.

"You got your Bogle," he said, looking at the TV with complete lack of comprehension, "and your Fleger. With me that's maybe forty to thirty-five percent. Like I want to kill people sometimes, Lester goes ahead. He's Bogle-Bogle. But if he was Bogle-Bogle-somebody else—the *right* somebody else—he might not. Like I'm Bogle-Fleger. But not *only*. Bogle-Fleger alone says 'Charlie Manson.' But you know who doesn't? Bogle-Fleger-*Lansing*-McGavin-Slate-Holliman. My benefit from when I was twelve . . . And *that's* the extra percent, because you got 3.0 Lansing, 2.0 Widmark, 2.5 Lancaster, maybe 1.0 Larry Storch. Maybe about point five Dorothy Provine. And Frank Faylen, who's the same guy as on 'Frasier.' That's what got me through. It's like . . . pointillism. The dots when you're twelve or so are the deepest. Almost blotches. That's why I'm bester than Lester. Sterling Fleeger-beeger, Lester Bestervester."

"Honey, you bester— you better rest," said Valerie.

"But you're not writing it down." His head flopped my way. "Neither are you."

"We're getting it in general," I said.

"Not the *numbers*, though; nobody's ever given out the numbers," he pleaded, weak on his pillow, desperate to get his message to the world. "The figs. Science will thank us."

So while Sterling went over it again, Valerie recorded the values. So much for this guy, so much for that guy. It really was kind of interesting. I hadn't realized how many influences he'd had. He came up with people I never would have suspected: Vito Scotti, Gene Evans, Sheb Wooley, Rafael Campos. He really was a conglomeration.

"Don't be too rigid," he warned us at the end. "You might have a couple points higher for a Beatle . . . Or once it's refined, you might find you say just one thing exactly like Bill Bixby. That's not reflected in the . . . We don't have sensitive enough . . . instruments . . . but basically, that's it. Robert Lansing. Lester . . . Lester . . ."

"Lester probably didn't get enough serotonin in his brain," I said.

"Lester didn't get enough nurturing," said Valerie.

"Coulda used some Brian Keith," said Sterling. "Settle him down." He suddenly registered dismay. "The kids today—don't have Lansing. Val . . . he has to be in there. Tell the parents. Tell the cable people."

He was getting agitated and moving too much, so we complimented him on his performance on the Strip. This diverted him. He nodded.

"Sometimes I hit a line just right, it's like, 'Dinngggggg . . . ' " He smiled beatifically.

It was hard to look at him, all busted up. Most of his injuries were due not to Lester's gunfire, but the impact of his landing.

"Ster," I asked him, "why in the hell didn't you double-puff when you were supposed to?"

He took a moment to comprehend the question and remember. Then he looked sheepish.

"Thinkin' about my lines," he said softly.

So by God, the answer was A.

CHAPTER SEVENTEEN

Last night on the Western Channel I saw an old "Gunsmoke" with Robert Lansing as special guest star.

When we were kids, Sterling liked that phrase; he liked the whole idea of the special guest star. It conjured up images of elegance and hospitality. He thought of special guest stars as a kind of fraternity of traveling pros, a loosely knit group like the Texas Rangers, moving from show to show, welcome everywhere. Lester Bogle, if he thought about them, probably disliked them for considering themselves better than the regular guest stars.

I sort of remembered this "Gunsmoke" episode, although I hadn't seen it in thirty-some years. It wasn't much of a part for Lansing. He had little to do besides smolder, sitting with his gang up in the rocks overlooking the stage station, threatening to wipe out all the passengers and half of Dodge City unless Matt Dillon released his brother.

Watching it this time, I not only knew how the story came out—I also knew how the actors and the original viewers came out. I first saw that episode with Sterling and Grandma Jessie. Robert Lansing, most of the "Gunsmoke" regulars and Grandma Jessie are gone, but Sterling and I have now reached a little rest stop on the road where we can stop and look around a bit.

Sterling may have a career after all. His New Year's performance led to a supporting role in Art Klee's new movie. The role, a hysterical cab driver, was tailored to his present inability to walk, and he finds it laughably easy. They apparently call him One-Take Fleger. He also intends, when on his feet, to return to the Actors' Bunker to play before audiences of five to thirty and be everybody again. Valerie Fassero has kept her job for the time being, so Sterling's okay financially until his acting pay increases. Valerie Fassero is crazy about him. I tell Abby she should act more like Valerie Fassero.

Lester lived to stand trial for the murder of Garland Bernard in his assault on the Mission Vista library. The verdict went against him in under an hour, with a later recommendation that he be executed. He is paralyzed below the waist from the gunshot wound he sustained in Las Vegas, and his mother intends to file suit against the Majestic Towers, Little Spudge-Face and the city of Las Vegas on his behalf.

Denny wasn't prosecuted because he never got around to doing anything. Lee Ann, his intended victim, entered 1997 with her gloom intact. I was with Sterling in the ICU when she came by the morning after and acknowledged that she had miscalculated about the end of the world.

"Maybe it wasn't your fault," Sterling suggested. "Maybe something came up and He had to be somewhere else."

"No; we were presumptuous." She looked around the room moodily. "I thought you were dead for sure. I guess the suit saved you."

"It's a good product," Sterling said.

Lee Ann looked from him to me and shook her head.

"Wally and the Beav," she said.

Loretta Bogle still has Denny and Dixie, and still calls Sterling on the phone, although he has managed to discourage her impromptu visits as a condition of the ten percent. She says now that she wishes she hadn't lived so much of her life for her family.

The Little Spudge-Face Company is thriving. There was some criticism of the whole New Year's episode as irrelevant to the typical child's experience, but no one could deny that the product performed. I mean, what a test. Now all we have to fight is the typical child's reluctance to wear it. Kids don't want to be encumbered. You have to chase Maggie from here to El Toro Road just to get the helmet on.

Elston survived his gunshot wound, but his marriage didn't. Joanne Petty disliked having to jockey for position with Claire Simon over his fallen body there on the street. Now he and Joanne are in protracted negotiations involving Bruyana.

He was very happy with Sterling's New Year's performance, however; it showed him the Spudge-Face spirit. He has even offered to let Sterling repeat the stunt next year.

Abby's CD, *Abby Zane,* is coming out this fall on the Splendid Wren label. I would particularly call your attention to "It Could Happen to You," "You Beat Me to the Punch" and "Now I Know."

Maggie is one of the brightest kids in her class at Remick Elementary. Her present teacher cites her sparkle and charisma, and says she can do anything when she applies herself.

On January 2, Sterling was flown back to Orange County, to McRae Memorial, for a splenectomy and reconstructive surgery. Mom met us back there. I picked her up at John Wayne and drove her around for a week. It was the first time she'd come out here; Abby and I had already taken Maggie to Illinois twice. Mom liked Laguna Beach. She read to Maggie and gave her some paints, and observed once again that Abby had straightened me out. She told Sterling she was proud of him for going back to what he wanted to do. She did mother and grandmother things for the entire week.

The day she arrived, she spent a few minutes alone with Sterling, and then asked to go somewhere with me alone. We sat at a table outside the Laguna Beach Hotel, at sunset, facing the ocean, and she handed me my adoption decree—whapped it down on the table between us.

"They were in the attic," she said. "This whole drama with your brother, and your medical emergencies . . . I thought, well, I'll find the things if they still exist. We weren't *supposed* to tell you, you know. But after forty years of badgering and the third degree . . ." She put her hands in her lap and tilted her head higher. "I gave Sterling his, and there's yours. So now you can do what you want. Hit the bricks. Do what you want. It's no concern of mine."

The decree was in its original envelope, mailed by Tasby & Buhl, Attorneys at Law, from Wheaton, the county seat in DuPage County, to Mr. and Mrs. Paul Fleger of Henley, Illinois. It had two three-cent stamps on it.

Inside was a three-page onion-skin document referring to Mom and Dad as the petitioners and me as the defendant and you, Irene Galowicz, as my mother. On this part of the decree, the heading, my name was Joseph Xavier Galowicz. I looked at it for a few moments before I realized that that name referred to me. Then I looked back up at yours.

"Irene Galowicz" carried no echoes for me. I have always liked the name "Irene," and the song "Goodnight, Irene," although that may just be because it's a good song. I was disappointed not to get a specific memory from seeing the name, but I guess it was just too long ago. Nothing lit up.

There were a couple paragraphs beginning "Now on this day comes the said PAUL R. FLEGER and RITA J. FLEGER . . ." and then six numbered paragraphs setting down the court's findings. Paragraph number four said you surrendered me to the Child Care Association on November 21, 1956, and gave them full authority to consent to my adoption.

Paragraph five: "That the petitioners have had custody of said minor child for a period of more than six months prior to the filing of said petition in this cause."

The paragraph after the numbered ones said, "IT IS THEREFORE ORDERED, ADJUDGED AND DECREED that henceforth and from the date hereof said child, Joseph Xavier Galowicz, to all legal intents and purposes, be the child of the petitioners, Paul R. Fleger and Rita J. Fleger, husband and wife respectively."

The last sentence on page three said, "It is further ordered, adjudged and decreed that the name of said child be changed from Joseph Xavier Galowicz to Adlai Jerome Fleger."

Then there was an attached page, stamped and signed by the county clerk, stating that all the above was legal and witnessed as of this 12th day of October, 1957.

After I read to the end, Mom flipped two pages back and tapped her finger on paragraph number six:

"That the petitioners are of sufficient ability to bring up said child and to furnish suitable support, maintenance and education for him."

"You've said some things about how we raised you," she said, referring, I guess, to remarks I made just out of junior college, "but we lived up to paragraph six."

She looked out over the ocean.

"As you know, my father—your grandfather—went down in the Depression," she said. "He couldn't fight through adversity. My mother and I were left. I was just out of college. At that time your father was the nicest guy, he was very sweet. The rest of his family didn't think so much of Mom and me, but he stuck by us. And by the time we found Sterling and you, we had chosen our path, and we didn't turn off it. We did *not* go under. We did *that*." She tapped paragraph six again, and then looked back out over the water, toward Catalina.

My mother is a little over five feet, with short gray hair that she likes to streak. She doesn't seem old. She's not a leading lady, more a friend of the heroine. She wears glasses and looks tired when she takes them off. She laughs when we tease her and says, "Oh, you." She's lost weight in the last year.

"Now we're done," she said. "And you have your own family. If you want to run out and find this woman, I'm sure you're welcome. Maybe you could have a whole new childhood. You should be discreet, though. She may not wish to be found."

I went to her side of the table and gave her a hug, which she waved off.

"When your father and I brought you and Sterling home," she said stiffly, "I always said those were the two happiest days of my life." She looked out, over the water. "Stevenson lost again, in between the two of you, but I didn't let it throw me."

I don't know; maybe Sterling didn't rate her high enough. We always loved Mom and all, but we tended to shrug her off too, as a gimme—something we just automatically deserved and got, like an elementary education with bus service back and forth. I never thought of her as a truly dominant influence, but as I look back, and as I look at myself, she stands out more.

I called Sterling's hospital room that night to compare decrees.

"Mine says Vincent Charles Bogle," he said. "But I also carry the influence of a long and varied theatrical tradition. What's your name? Is it Mary or Sue?"

"Turns out I'm Polish."

There was a brief pause, and then he said, "Can't say I'm surprised."

How about that? My first ethnic slur—from my own brother. I'm glad now I never made a social career out of telling those jokes, even though some of them were funny. I'd feel like I'd been spitting into the wind.

So that's how I got your name, and that's what's new with your old pal of so many years ago.

You may not be too happy with my mom for giving you away like that. I don't blame you if you're upset. But I think she did it for two reasons: one, she knew me well enough to know I wouldn't really run off to burst in on your life; and two, she was tidying up her affairs as regards Sterling and me, because she was ill. She's since started chemotherapy out here in California.

I wrote all this in January and February, without knowing where to send it. While I was writing, I was looking.

Abby got me a book called *Track 'Em Down*. It contains tips on how to find people, using different kinds of publicly available records. With persistence and these tips you can eventually find just about anyone. Abby felt we should try to locate you, if for no other reason than to ask those questions for Maggie, and I agreed. So many things are genetic now.

Anyway, not to make an opera out of it, we finally found you as the surviving daughter of Joseph Xavier Galowicz, who died in Racine, Wisconsin, in 1977. It was Sterling's long-shot idea that I might have been named after your father, and the Social Security Administration lists everybody who's died in the U.S. since 1962, along with the zip code where the death occurred. Eventually we got your married, or rather widowed, name, and an address to send this thing to.

(There's still a slim chance that after all this I've got the wrong Irene Galowicz. If so, of course you don't have to concern yourself about my request for medical information; just disregard it.)

As I go over what I'm sending, it occurs to me that you might take it as a giant insult—or at least, that part where I said we didn't have to meet. You may think I envision you as a Loretta Bogle. That's not so; I really don't suppose you'd be anything like what Sterling drew. But I think his story does illustrate what you might call the other side of the family reunion picture.

You see a lot of grown adoptees on TV nowadays, having emotional meetings with their birth parents. But I've learned from Sterling's experience that these get-togethers aren't all successful. Some folks just don't hit it off, blood or not.

And some people might not care to go back all those years and turn themselves inside out. I wouldn't blame you if you didn't. After all, you moved on, and I grew up. We even both have different names now. I'd feel bad if the only result of my contacting you was to remind you of a painful time.

At one point I thought, Well, I'll just send a simple request for medical information for Maggie, and leave out the rest. But that seemed curt, and it didn't correspond to how I felt. I really wanted to tell you all this, about me and Sterling, and Abby, and of course Maggie. And Abby said you might like to hear that I had turned out all right.

(I hope you weren't disappointed to learn just how I *did* turn out. I mean, I know I'm not a doctor. But it could have been worse, believe me; anybody who knew me in my twenties would tell you.)

Anyway, I finally decided to send the whole thing. I realize it's a bit newsy; if we ever correspond further I'll keep it under two pages.

As for where we go from here: If you'd prefer not to respond, well, we're no worse off than we were before. Maggie can get along with regular checkups. If you'd like to pass on that medical information, that would be wonderful. In fact I'd love to read whatever you care to send. And if you want to meet, I'm game. We could pick a neutral ground if you wanted; have a kind of no-obligation dinner. I'd buy. Can't say fairer than that.

I don't know if I put this in anywhere, so I'll

say it now: I don't question the decision you made, in 1956. I know you acted for the best. Bad things happen to little kids sometimes, but I was lucky, and I think you arranged for me to be. That's why I especially want you to know that things turned out okay on this end.

Well, the late talk shows are on and tomorrow's a workday. I guess I'm finally at an end.

No matter what I call myself, I know that inside me you carry one of the big numbers Sterling spoke of. And although you and I don't know each other, we were once very close. So in signing off I'm going to take another liberty and address you informally. I have to step around the word "Mom," as it's been taken, but I would like to say: Greetings from your long-ago baby, and from Abby, and from Maggie, who may look familiar to you, and from me again, all grown, and with that I'll say good night, Irene.